Pain In Love

Julia Osmond

Contents

1. Their life

U pon hearing the door the getting opened I quickly sat upright

It was my so called husband gosh i can't believe I am married that too with this jerk

Well at first I was excited to be with him but all that changed when...

"You are a fool to think I accepted this marriage because I like you or something like that let me clear it to you the only feeling I feel towards you is hate and nothing else

And if you think marrying me will do you any good then you are mistaken dear samaira, this marriage will mark your journey to the hell

Welcome to my hell Samaira Sweetheart"

The way he told sweetheart that day gave me butterflies in the stomach, and not good kind of

After that talk with him I tried to cancel my wedding but like a bastard my father is he only cares about money and I know this jerk right here gave my father a lots of money in exchange of me

"Tsk tsk first day of our marriage and you are already asking for punishment" he said with a sadistic smile

I frowned in confusion, punishment but I didn't even do anything

"I have been calling you for past 5 minutes but look at you lost in your own dreamland" his tone was somewhat between serious and sarcastic

"What do you want?" I asked irritated

"Now that's not the tone to talk with your husband" he said with a smirk

"I can say the same thing to you" I retorted

I gulped my saliva after seeing his face it's like in minutes he go possessed by some devil, he looked fucking pissed

In a minute he came near the bed and hurled me up by my neck, I didn't do anything it would be good if he choked me to death

"You are my wife learn to respect me" he spit out in anger

"Respect is earned not forced on someone, and till now you haven't done anything which will make me respect you" I said loud enough for him to hear it

Shit samaira, looks like you want to die on the first day of your marriage itself, his anger just got more fueled by what I said

―――――――――

Gosh another tiring day, sometimes I wish I wasn't a daughter in law of such a rich family

Suddenly someone barged into the room, well who else can come other than him

"Do you need something" I asked while putting on my robe of the night-gown

When he didn't answered I looked at him only to find him looking at my legs which were visible due to my nightgown

I snapped my fingers infront of him and asked again "do you need anything"

If I remember correctly he said not to enter in his room without his permission and look at him entering my room like he owns it, basically he does but it's my room and doesn't matter

"Come in my room I need to find some of my files" oh did I said that even though I am not allowed in room I still need to clean it along with his study room that's on the same floor we are living

Can't believe all the brothers have separate floor for themselves

"Will you come or you have became a statue over there" he asked irritation lacing in his voice

"Coming"

"Here is your file" with that I started walking out when he stopped me, "from now on you will sleep here with me" and with that I really got butterflies in my stomach do he really want to take our relationship to next level, I couldn't help but feel butterflies flutter inside of me

"Don't feel too happy it's for the image sake not for you" and there goes my happiness...

____

What a day, I thought while removing my jewellery and keeping them in their respective box

He was sitting on the bed working on his laptop even though he eyes were on the screen I could feel it on my back

Gosh Disha you are dreaming again, he is Ryan raghuvanshi the man who doesn't likes you one bit and can't even look at you, he will never look at you, let alone so hard that you can feel his gaze

I took my clothes for the night which was a silky night gown, and closed the bathroom door behind me

After changing, I came out with my heavy work saree hanging on my hand, wedding can be tiresome, especially if it's your devar's wedding

I started folding my saree just the way it was until I heard his voice

"Get me my red file" he said, his voice like ice

I nodded and kept my saree in the wordrobe and bought him the file he asked for

After completing my night duties I slept with a thought that occurs my mind everytime

Why do I have to be in such a marriage?

———————

2. You have an Affair??

D ISHA

Another day, another useless ray of hope gosh I just hope one day I can be free from this

Then I remembered why I have truly married the great Ryan Raghuvanshi and all my hope to be free from this marriage just vanishes into thin air

I was a middle class girl with a handicapped mom and two younger siblings, I used to work two jobs to provide for all of us

That's when he came in my life like a knight in shining armour only if I knew at that time that he was nothing like that

He kept a proposal infront of me, I should marry and in return he would take care of my family

I was reluctant at first but my mom told to accept it, and therefore I did

At first I thought he was cold and closed off but I can work on him I can get close to him but no he was always like that and it was me who just foolishly kept falling in love with him

I still he remember what he said on our first day of marriage

"I may have married you but this is just for namesake don't expect anything from this" his voice like always as cold as ice

I never understood that why did he even marry me then, if it was just a namesake marriage then just why?

"Disha bhabhi everyone is calling you downstairs" Kritika came and informed me and broke my trance

"I am coming" saying this I started getting ready for the day, setting for something simple I decided to go with a mint coloured dress

Upon reaching the dining table, it was like everyday, all serious and brooding

I sat down beside my husband like everyone else

"Today ma and my baby is coming make sure everything is at place" Ryan spoke with authority

"Baby, don't tell me you have an extra marital affair" Samaira boomed and everyone chocked, yeah everyone was drinking orange juice including me

"What shit are you talking samaira learn to control you fucking mouth" Rudransh said rather harshly I might add

"No samaira these three have a younger sister and they call her baby affectionately" Kritika explained

"Thanks bhabhi I am glad somebody knows how to talk unlike some other people" she said indirectly taunting Rudransh, and he gave her a look which indicated he was pissed

God, the day has not even started and everybody is at each other's neck

"If you all don't mind I would like everyone to finish their breakfast today itself" This time it was raghav, the one who spoke the least among the brothers

After that everyone got silent and focused on finishing their meals

Like always Ryan was the first one to get up and then his brothers following him

"I am sorry bhabhi for what I said earlier it would have surely hurted you, it was stupid of me to do such a thing" Samaira said

"It's nothing dear, besides it's not like we have any feelings or this marriage mean something"

That's a big fatass lie and I think we know that, my sub conscious mocked me

Atleast it's true at his side, I fired back

"What do you mean by that?" Samaira asked confused

"Ahh that can be a talk for another day let's get on with our chores, and let me tell you our mother in law is very strict in terms of completing our chores" I dismissed the subject while leaving the atmosphere a little less tensed

———————

"Bhabhi" a chirpy voice caught my attention and made me hault my chores in the middle

"Saanvi" I smiled at her

"Where are my other two SIL especially Ansh's Bhai wife, couldn't come in the wedding yesterday" she queried, in her happy voice

"First tell me where is mom, I should probably meet her first" I asked

"Mom is sleeping and she said not to disturb her for another two to three hours, now come take me to my other two SIL" she practically dragged me outside the kitchen

"Okay okay no need to drag me they both are in the backyard let's go"

Soon enough we reached the backyard of our- sorry his house

"There they are" hearing my voice they both turned towards me and kritika's face immediately curved into a smile

"Saanvi, so glad you finally came" she came and engulfed saanvi in a hug

"Saanvi as in the those three idiots, asshole and biggest jerk in the world sister" samaira commented and all three of us had wide eyes, because of what she just said

"What did you just said, you good for nothing girl" A voice roared behind us and it didn't took me long enough to guess it was....

____

3. Orthodox beliefs

"Leave my bloody hands" I said jerking my hands away from his hold, he had a fucking grip of a gorilla

While I was examining my hand for any type of bruises, he suddenly grabbed me by shoulders and pulled towards himself, due to the force I collided with his chest and stood back in my place.. which was just mere inches away from him

Our damn noses were literally touching due it, our glaring contest came to an end by him asking

"What did you just said about my me and brothers"

"Umm maybe what I think is truth" I replied with an equally agitated tone

"Rudransh don't do anything with her let her g.." he stopped disha bhabhi by just showing his hand

"You think you can stay in our house and fucking curse us" he growled

"Yeah do you have fricking problem with it because the last time I checked it wasn't me who wanted to be here" I scoffed

He again gripped my arms ohh God it hurts so bad

"Rudransh leave me you are hurting me" I said squirming in his hold

"That's enough of childish behaviour for today ansh leave her right this instant" A authoritive voice behind me said

His hands immediately came down and I turned around to see who had the power to make even the Rudransh 'the asshole' obey

"Dadi I didn't knew you were coming too Ryan didn't told me" Disha bhabhi said and touched her feet, Kritika bhabhi following her trail too

Sensing I should do the same thing I quickly touched her feet

"I told him not too" she replied, authority was oozing from her voice, no wonder she is their grandma

"As for you young man is this the way you should treat a woman, moreover your wife" she asked him

"But dadi-" just like he shutted off bhabhi dadi did it the same way, finally a sensible person in the house

"Save your excuses, this is the last time I am seeing a behaviour like this in my house, understood" she said and I can see how he nodded his head, unwillingly

"Maa you woke up you should have woken up me too" another unfamiliar voice came and for the second time I turned around to come face to face with another stunning woman

Again the same thing touching her feet

"What was happening here I heard shouting" his mother asked

"Ask your son looks like he have forgotten the manners we have given him" Saying this dadi left the room

"Disha what was maa talking about" and disha bhabhi started telling everything that happened

"So because of you my son got to hear so many things from maa" hearing this I came to a conclusion, this house is full of idiots

"Your son got scolded because of his behaviour not because of me" I said calmly but I was anything but calm

"You how dare you, you are just a middle class girl who just knows how to entrap rich guys like my son" her voice as cold as ice

Even though I don't want to admit but it hurts, I mean anyone would get hurt I am a human afterall

"Mom" I expected this from my so called husband but guess he already left the room, it was saanvi

"How can you such things to bhabhi" even though I have just met her she seems pretty decent compared to the rest

"You don't come in between these" "I will mom the language you are speaking is highly unacceptable"

Seeing there is no reason to stay thereI left the living room, not even one day in this house and there is so much trouble, I am already contemplating divorcing that arrogant cocky bastard.

I am in the kitchen right now deciding what to do, as it's my pehli rasoi I do have to make something today as per the ritual

Right on the cue I heard footsteps heading into the kitchen, turning I saw it was disha bhabhi

"I am sorry for what happened earlier" "it's not even your fault"

"I just can't believe two ladies from the same house can be so different"

"Yeah dadi is more of open minded than maa as she comes from a orthodox family and even though she got married is such a family and her mother in law was open minded she never changed she still believes in that old saying 'pati parmashwar' and expect her daughter in laws to treat her sons like a god"

"How do you know all this" I couldn't help but ask

"1 year in this house has teached me enough, I have gone through the same phase as you as I was also not enough to be in her class" She said smiling lightly but I am not a fool to not understand it, it's the same smile I use to hide my pain

"So bhabhi can you tell me where are all the ingredients to make kheer" I asked changing the topic

"Oh yes today would be your pehli rasoi I totally forgot come I will help you

"Hey don't forget me" kritika bhabhi joined us and we three took of to work

#####

"Well done kiddo" kritika bhabhi said after tasting my kheer

"I am not a kid" I whined

"How old are you" she asked

"I am 23 turning 24 soon" "well I am 25 and disha bhabhi 26 so you are a kiddo indeed"

Like every good time comes to an end our devil of a mother in law called seeing the time we understood it's dinner time and everyone is seated

"You both go ahead I will come with the kheer" I told them and they both nodded with the food

I took out the kheer for everyone in a bowl and smirked to myself, time to teach lesson to my dear mother in law and hubby

I won't let anyone get away by disrespecting me I took the salt and sprinkle it generously in two bowls specially

After that I took the tray to serve everyone, I kept the kheer beside everyone's plate and sat down with mine

As childish it sounds, I was excited for what would happen next

#####

So guys how was the chappy??

Which couple do you like the most??

Isn't their mother in law a total bitch??

Thoughts on dadi and saanvi??

Don't forget to vote and comment??

Angel..

4. Everything is wet

S AMAIRA

Everyone started eating, including me with my eyes on them to see their reactions

As expected my dearest mother in law shrieked as soon as she ate the first spoon

"What is this who puts salt in kheer" she fumed and particularly glaring at me

By now everyone was looking at me, "I didn't do anything" I said as innocently as possible

By now the jerk has eaten too but he didn't do or say anything but was just glaring in my direction with me returning it in same intensity

Soon everyone got up and went in their respective room

I was washing my hand when somebody took my hands and spun me around

"What the heck" I shouted at the intruder

"The stunt you pulled today Mrs raghuvanshi is appreciating but alas if you thought you would get away with it because the trouble for you would doubled now, good luck" with that he left

Great just great, and here I was thinking my quota for the day was over, gosh living here is just like living in a daily soaps

I quickly washed my hands and made my way towards his room.

He was working on his laptop with his glasses on. Looks hot on him though, gosh Samaira get out of that gutter please

I went into the closet and took my nightsuit, and quickly changed into it

Upon coming out I noticed something this room had two different beds it wasn't here yesterday, anyways it's good don't have to sleep with that jerk

When I reached near bed, I noticed another thing the bed was fucking wet

"What is it, why is it wet" I asked angrily

"How will I know" he didn't even looked up, how rude

Well he isn't the gentleman of the year now is he??.

Sometimes I think how my subconscious can be so smart

I am fucking tired and this son of a-No use of cursing his mother

After roaming my eyes around the room it landed on the couch, perfect it can definitely fit me

I took new blanket and pillow from the cupboard made my way towards it

As soon as I sat down I shrieked what the hell this wet too, just great I will strangle this bastard to death

God, I can't stand this man now who is so heartless where will sleep now

I heard shuffling, looks like his work got done, "where will I sleep" I asked straight to the point

"I don't know nor I give a fuck now switch off the lights and let me fucking sleep I have work unlike you" he barked and it hurts my pride but I was a little hurt

Who talks in that way, looks like dadi's scolding wasn't enough

"I would like to sleep NOW" he screamed

I switched off the lights and went into the balcony, there I saw a swing, pretty big to fit me, I sat down on it

Bastard, after seeing his mother now I know where he got it from

Sighing I looked up at the sky, so clear and empty, nothing was present there, just like my life I couldn't help but compare

Yawning, my eyes slowly started dropping, goodnight to myself

#####

KRITIKA

Today was eventful, I knew that samaira is nothing like me or disha bhabhi, while we choose to stay silent here she took her stand

"Kritika" Raghav's voice bought me back into reality

"Yeah"

"Tomorrow be ready we have been invited to a Mr and Mrs Chaudhary anniversary"

"Just not me" I said timidly

"Did you said something" he asks coldly and that alone made me head nod in negetive

"Tell this to disha bhabhi and samaira too" saying this he went to sleep, I am sure he will get paralysed if he spoke more than few words with me, i thought

God I am tired, changing in my sleepwear I slept on my side of the bed with my back facing him

Gosh how I wish things would be different between us but no my uncle always have to ruin it for me, no it's not like I hate him he is the best thing that happened in my life but only if he didn't forced me and him in this marriage then atleast I would have lived my life peacefully

I just wish either my husband starts loving me back just like I do or I get free from this marriage..

#####

So guys how was it??

Drop your comments

Angel..

5. A kiss? maybe not

KRITIKA

Soft rays of sunlight broke my peaceful slumber, I looked beside me to see he was already up and getting ready, like usual

I got up from my bed and went in the washroom to freshen up by the time I came out freshning up he already left, I huffed, this man is just a stone

Can't even exchange morning pleasantries with his goddamn wife

Getting ready in my simple salwar kameez I went downstairs in the puja Ghar to do my daily thing

Upon reaching there I saw dadi was already there, I quitely greeted her and went on with my daily Puja

After that I went in the kitchen to help the other two and serve breakfast to everyone

"Today is Mr and Mrs Chaudhary anniversary and he has invited all of us" Ryan Bhai said, god everyone belonging from this family has such a authoritive voice

"I hate going to parties" Sanvi groaned

Me too dear me too

"I know my baby but going to this party is important he is our biggest investors anyways everyone has to be ready by 7" saying this everyone went quite

Why do I have to go, the company is managed by Ryan Bhai and Rudransh, my husband doesn't even work there he is a architecture for godsakes

#####

At sharp 6 three sarees were delivered at the raghuvanshi's mansion, yeah one for each daughter-in-law

According to our sweet mother in law we have no taste or class and we could never match them so it's better if her sons buy our dresses whenever we have a party to attend, her words not mine

But I admit everytime I get stunned to see the saree he certainly has a great taste, who knows if he even buys it or not, his assistant always buys it

Leaving my thoughts aside I started getting ready because Ryan Bhai is surely punctual if he said be ready by 7 then you better be otherwise he won't hesitate to leave you here alone

I wore my red satin saree, satin sarees are always my enemy gosh it always slips from my hands, I need disha bhabhi

I took my phone and quickly dialed for her, "hello bhabhi come in my room fast" saying this I ended

My back was facing the door and then disha bhabhi entered the room, "bhabhi see na this satin saree is not getting pleated please help me na" I said

I waited for few minutes, why was bhabhi not helping me i turned around to come face to face with himBlood instantly rushed to my cheeks

I was just standing in my underskirt and blouse "you"

Suddenly he started coming closer and on instinct I started going backwards

Suddenly my legs stopped due to something, the bed, he was standing mere centimetres away now

He started learning closer and automatically my lips parted anticipating his next move, I know my instinct should be to push him away but come on I am sure if he is your husband you would never push him away

I thought something happen now but nothing happened he simply took the saree from my hand and started wrapping it around, expertly I might add

In few minutes he was done with the saree and I couldn't help but stare at him in awe, but wait a second how did he learn it does he have a girlfriend and he does it for her

I couldn't help but feel jealous and a little hurt at this thought

He finally tucked one last pin in the saree and stepped back, "learn how wear a saree or no need to wear it" He said harshly and went inside the walk in closet

How rude! Can't he atleast speak politely, and here I thought he was going to kiss me some moments back

#####

"So sorry kritika I know you called me but maa and dadi both needed me" disha bhabhi said as soon as I stepped into the living room

"It's okay bhabhi I managed" I said not mentioning that incident

"How am I looking bhabhi" Samaira asked as soon as she came down

"Pretty like always" I said and disha bhabhi nodded in agreement

We all three are wearing satin sarees like me samaira also added a belt in her saree

All the men came down and just I now I noticed him and I were matching not just me but all couples were matching

"I hope everyone is ready to go" Ryan Bhai asked and we all nodded

Indicating we should start heading towards our car that's what we all did while dadi, maa and saanvi took one car all the couples took their own separate car

After what happened in the room I was pretty flustered and to think I would travel with him alone had me blushing scarlet.

"I would like to reach the party today itself" his annoyed voice bought me back into reality, I quickly got into the car sat as far as possible from him

The driver started driving and moving towards our destination,

"Today is an important event I don't want you to mess it anyway" he ordered in his usual distant voice

Like I ever mess it up, the daughter-in-laws of raghuvanshi are more like robots

Always be beside your husband and always smile standing beside him, fake or real doesn't matter , always give the media a impression that the relationship with your husband is best in the whole world when in reality it's the total opposite

Always be a social butterfly, keep your posture straight behave like a lady, do this do that, and the list just goes on

Because one thing I learnt, Media and reporters are like a butterfly and Raghuvanshi's like a flower wherever they go they follow them so never give them a chance to question their pride, the Raghuvanshi name

The sudden hault broke my chain of thoughts

He went out first and didn't even opened the door for me, what a meanie!

The driver did it for me and upon coming out I saw our family cats looks like everyone has arrived before us

Media were like swarm of bees they were everywhere and the flashes of camera were literally blinding me

He gave me his arms to take, like all other fake shows

I took his arms with a smile and started walking towards the door, I am sure by now reporters would have taken 100 of photos of us.

Inside there were no reporters thank god as now there is no need to hold hands he jerked his hands away from rather harshly I might add

Sensing he doesn't want me near him I quickly scanned the room for my other family members

Samaira, saanvi and disha bhabhi were standing near the corner, I made my way towards them

"Where is maa and dadi?" I asked

"Dadi was not feeling well so they are in one of the room they will come down once it's time for cake cutting" Samaira said

We four talked for some time, suddenly my throat felt dry, "guys I am coming in few seconds"

Saying this I left for the bar, reaching there I ordered a water and mocktail

As I was waiting for my drink I suddenly felt someone's hand on my bare waist, I quickly jumped back from the contact

Seeing the intruder I came face to face with Mr Chaudhary's son, Aadarsh, he is handsome man too bad now he has stooped this low to touch someone without their permission

"What the hell Mr Chaudhary don't you have some manners that you shouldn't touch woman inappropriately" I seethed

"Oh come on now don't be like you don't enjoy it I certainly know women like you first you try to seduce us and then act innocent like you weren't seducing us in the first place" he said, with a smirk

"If you think you know us women then you are very wrong because not all women try to seduce everyone, and me seducing a bastard like you it won't even happen even if you payed me" I screamed, I am sure by now everyone is hearing us

"You bitch you called me a bastard" he went to slap me but my reflexes were quick

I quickly held his hands and kneed him in the crotch

"KRITIKA" A voice boomed as soon as Aadarsh fell on floor due to pain

Someone grabbed my forearm, and this certain someone was none other than Raghav Raghuvanshi.

######

So guys how was the chapter??

Any thoughts on raghav and kritika I tried to make whole chapter on them

Next chapter it would be Disha and Ryan

Angel...

6. A Game Of Truth And Dare

KRITIKA

"What the fuck do you think you are doing?" He gritted out lowly

"What am I doing this scum here tried harrassing me" I said glaring at that good for nothing jerk

"Apologise to him right now" he said shocking me to the core

"What"

"Don't make me repeat myself" he said

"I am not at fault I won't apologise" I stood on my ground

"This is unacceptable Raghav how can your wife hit my son" Mr Chaudhary chipped in

"Why don't you ask your son what he did?" I retorted

"I did nothing dad I was just trying to talk to her and she hit me" I gasped, the audacity of this man to lie through his teeth

"Kritika I won't repeat again, APOLOGISE TO HIM" Tears pooled in my eyes because of his harsh tone

"Wow without even listening to me you are already telling me to apologise, like I said before I WON'T "

"What's happening here" Ryan Bhai voice resonated

I looked towards him to see my all family members standing there, I quickly ran towards Disha bhabhi and she held me in her arms

"What happened kritika" When she asked this I broke into loud sobs

"It's not my fault why everyone is telling me to apologise" I cried

"Disha and samaira take kritika home" Ryan Bhai said

Soon we exited the venue with me still hiccuping something I do a lot after crying

After sitting into the car, samaira asked, "bhabhi can you tell now what happened but only if you want to"

Then I told them everything, and by end samaira looked ready to jump out of car and end his life

"How dare that bastard do that and lie after it and I can believe raghav Bhai believe some nobody over his wife"

A bitter laugh left my lips hearing that "he would surely believe someone over me samaira because here I am the nobody in his life" I said sadly, after I said that silence fell upon the car

#####

I was removing my jwellery when I heard the door opening and closing and footsteps following after

"Do you know what you did today you messed up everything for Ryan's Bhai company" anger was radiating from his voice but even I was seething

Turning I met his eyes daringly, "If stopping a man from trampling my dignity is wrong then I am very proud of it and why should I explain anything to you when you will always believe others over me" saying this I left for changing my clothes

Coming out from the corner of eyes I saw he wanted to talk but I wasn't in the damn mood so I quickly layed down on bed with quilt covering me and switched off the bedside lamp on mide side.

#####

DISHA

"She should have apologized now my Ryan's company will suffer consequences because of that arrogant girl" I swear to god sometimes I contemplate putting poison in my mother's in law food

Ignoring her comment about kritika I went upstairs to see if kritika is up or not by this time she is usually up and in the kitchen beside me

Not like I want her to work, I am just worried that's it

When I entered her room she didn't even noticed me just staring into blank space

I stood beside her and gently shook her it looks like she was in a trance

"Bhabhi what are you doing here" she asks

"Well kritika I came to call you downstairs come quickly everyone is waiting at the dining table" Informing her I went downstairs

As expected kritika was the last one to join us at the table

As soon as kritika sat down, Ryan cleared his throat to get everyone's attention

"Yesterday I got Mr Chaudhary's call and whatever kritika did-" Kritika piped in

"Ryan Bhai whatever I did yesterday was right and if you are also telling me to apologise to that douchebag then sorry I won't do it" She finished

"No I was going to say that indeed whatever you did was right and the server who was making your drink in the bar yesterday told him everything and he said sorry to you" Ryan finished

A look of relief was on kritika's face and even though raghav is good at hiding emotions he looked somewhat regretful

I just hope there won't be anymore drama... atleast for now

#####

"Bhabhi let's do it na"

"For the tenth time saanvi my answer is still no"

"But why"

"Because that game is stupid" I said

"Kritika and samaira bhabhi atleast you both say yes" "only if disha bhabhi says yes"

Right now she is bugging us to play truth and dare with her, I never liked that game, don't know why

When I looked over to where saanvi was sitting and she was no longer there

"Where she went" I asked the other two

"I think she went upstairs" nodding my head I once again started doing my dishes

Once we three were done with our work, kritika said

"Let's sit in the lawn for sometime today is full moon's day" agreeing we all started heading towards the lawn, which is situated in the other side of the mansion

One thing I love about this lawn is the way it is decorated, absolutely beautiful

There are sofas to sit there and a small table situated in the middle with small lamps illuminating the whole lawn

"Bhabhi see whom I bought here" suddenly a voice startled me

"Gosh saanvi you scared-" my voice hitched seeing who was was standing behind her

All the brothers

"Now as you all are free let's play the game"she said, excitement dripping from her voice

"And no one can back out now" saying this she and her brothers settled on other sofa and just like that saanvi spinned the bottle

It landed on samaira and me, "so disha bhabhi truth or dare"

"Truth" I answered

"Tell us about your first love" her question shocked me

"Come on bhabhi tell us who is it, is it Ryan Bhai or someone else" saanvi asked excitedly

For split second my eyes met with him but I averted it quickly

"No your brother is not my first love" I said

"Then who is it" saanvi again asked

"Harsh Raichand, we met in college and you know what was the best thing he and I were dating but then on graduation day he left and never came back and with that l also left the hope for him to come back and continue our relationship and then I got married with your brother" I completed I again looked in his direction and for some reason he has jaw clenched along with his fists

Even after so many years his name bought a smile on my face, sure I loved Ryan now but harsh was and always will be my first love

And just like this the game went on until it landed on me again

"Okay bhabhi again truth or dare"

"Truth"

"Describe us your first kiss" After this I literally choked on the air

#####

So how was the chapter??

Any thoughts on raghav and kritika??

What about disha and Ryan

I couldn't make any scene for third couple but it would come for sure

Next chapter would be different....... It would be in male lead pov guess which one??

Next update would be uploaded after vote target is completed

Target : 70 votes

7. Virgin?

DISHA

As soon as that question left her, my whole body turned red, what type of question was that and how am I supposed to answer that, It's a little embarassing thing to say

Contemplating what to say I decided to come up with a simple, "No I haven't had it yet"

"Aww our bhabhi is so sweet see how is she blushing" Samaira chuckled,

As she was sitting beside me I quitely pinched her, "oww what was that for" she said rubbing her arm

Leaning in her i whispered in her ear "You shut up right now cause the next time your turn will be up I am sure you won't like it" I said with a smile

"I think it's enough for today anyways I am sleepy I am going to sleep" She said and went inside

"Yeah I think now everyone should go to sleep as it's late already" saying this I also went inside

God I will never play that game again, this is the exact reason I never play it even though I know it is not necessary to always say the truth but what can I say I am bad at lying

I reached his room I can never call this room mine this room contains nothing that I can call mine expect the few clothes I bought with me other than everything is given to me by raghuvanshi's

I took my night wear and stripped myself out of my clothes and wore it and left my clothes in the laundry basket

I was making the bed when suddenly a hot breath fanned my neck and a hand wrapped them around my waist

"Ryan" I breathed out what is he doing

I turned around, his hand still around me as soon as I did it I was hitted with a strong smell of alcohol

"Ryan what are you doing leave me" I say wiggling in his hold

"Stay still" by now I was sure he was fully under the influence of alcohol

But aren't people supposed to be weak in that state why he has such a strong hold on me then

"Do you love me?" He question caught me off guard

"What"

"Are you deaf?"

Even though I don't know if he would remember it by tomorrow I know this my chance to tell him what my heart is longing to do for so long

"Yes" I said while staring into his amber eyes

As soon as I said that he took face in between his rough colloused palms and claimed my lips in a rough kiss

My eyes widened, my first kiss with my husband and I would be lying if i said it didn't felt good, sparks were flying in my entire body

His hands started roaming on my entire body, then it clicked me he is doing all this because he is drunk and he won't remember it tomorrow, and even if I want this it would probably not right I don't want my first time to be like this

Placing my hands on his chest I slightly pushed him away, he pulled back with a groan

"Ryan stop it"

"Why should I stop I am your husband and you just now told me you love me then why don't you want it?"

"Because now you under the influence of alcohol and I don't want you to regret anything" I huffed

He again snaked his arms around and as much as I try to resist it his wood and forest smell really did something to my insides

Shaking my head and clearing it, I once again tried to remove his hands, because one of us has to be responsible here

"Ryan try to understand" I whimpered

"You don't want to be with me because I am drunk or you are still in love with that boy you mentioned" His eyes were dark and gulped, he looked intimidating

But wait do I sense jealousy there, haha disha keep dreaming, my subconscious mocked me

"Tell me" he screamed, geez even though I like this Ryan more he is more scary like this

"You are misunderstanding Ryan I am saying this for you only because you would regret" I say knowing very well he would regret it in the morning and even though every cell and fibre in my body is saying to jump on him but I won't do it

"Then I won't regret it" saying this he kissed me with so much force we both fell on the bed with him on top of me

Come on disha this is your chance it's not a everyday occurance that your husband the great Ryan Raghuvanshi is ravishing you in the bed, enjoy this while it lasts you bitch, with this every single rational and sane thought flew through the window

"Kiss me back"

"I don't know how" "just do as I do"

He again started kissing me this time me following his lead we both started roaming our hands on each other body with my hands tangled in his hairs and his hands exploring my body

Breaking the kiss he started moving down till he reached my neck and started sucking there, I didn't even noticed he has already removed my nightsuit and I was just in my garments

His hands went behind my back and unclasped my bra and I lifted my back a little to help him remove it

He groaned after seeing my breasts and I sub consciously covered my breasts thinking it's not okay

"Don't hide them from me baby" he took my hands away and pinned them both down with his and dipped down to suck my right breast

I let out low moan, "ahh"

He kept on sucking my nipples, he let go off my left hand and started massaging left breast, after some time switching the nipples

Now I couldn't stop my moans from falling, "oh god" I arched my back pushing breasts into him more

I felt his hands travelling down to south right into my panties which were wet due to the pleasure he is giving me

"You are so fucking wet" he said while his hands were circling my clit and I bucked my hip at the sensation

He bought his face near mine and kissed me passionately while slipping one of his fingers in my slit

I moaned in both pain and pleasure, he breaked the kiss and breathed near my ear, "you are so tight"

His second fingers joined in the first one both going at a rhythmic pace and I felt some knotting in my stomach

I closed my eyes as I felt myself closer to coming and his pace of the fingers increasing

"Come all on my fingers wifey" hearing him say that was the last straw and came hard and for a moment everything became white before me

When I came back into the world there he was licking his fingers clean which was inside of me few minutes back

I blushed from roots of my hair till the tip of feet, I felt shy all of sudden and i couldn't look into his eyes anymore

He took my chin inbetween his fingers and forced me to look in his eyes

"No no wifey no being shy we have a long night ahead of us" he said his breath fanning my face, I didn't noticed when ne became naked but now his manhood was poking at my entrance

And I suddenly became concious, I am losing my virginity, I am going to have sex and then I won't be virgin anymore

Many questions surrounded me like will it hurt? Does it really feel that good as people say? Am I ready for this?

"Don't worry I will go slow" his voice brings me back to my reverie

"Are you a virgin?" He asks and I nodded

"Me too" I looked at him shocked, I didn't thought he would be a virgin too he literally has sex appeal oozing off him

But on the other hand I was happy I am his first and most probably his last too just like he was mine

We both made eye contact and then he asked, "can I?" And I nodded with a, "yes"

He again positioned himself at my entrance and slipped his tip only and I clutched his shoulders, I was slightly uncomfortable but nevertheless motioned him go further, I won't back out now

Inch by inch he went inside of pussy until he was fully inside, my insides slightly burn at the intrusion and little tears sprang in my eyes

He remained still as I waited for the pain to subsidue, once I was sure I nodded for him to move

"Faster Ryan" my pain was long gone and now I was screaming in pleasure

"Fuck yeah" he grunted

He took my ankle and placed my right leg on his shoulder to get better access , god he was so deep

He kept going in and out at a faster pace and my insides were trembling with need of orgasm, he leaned in and took my lips in his

"You feel so good" he groaned and moaned when I feel him hitting that right spot

I feel close to my orgasm again for the second time in night, he took my fingers and interlaced his with mine while laying on top of me and going with his long hard strokes

His two long hard thrust and that all took me to fall apart in his arms with orgasm over taking my body and he following behind soon after

Grunting he emptied himself inside of me with me clenching around him making him drop every last bit of come inside me

I moaned a little as his cock slipped outside and he fell beside me with his come running down my leg along with my juices

He took me in his arms with his arms around my back and my head on his shoulder

Before I could say something to him, he was already sound asleep, I sighed and laid my head on his chest and hearing his heartbeat

But my mind already dreading tomorrow......

######

So.... Something just got steamy here

Did you like it??

Which Ryan do you like the mostOur normal Ryan or drunk one??

Comment your thoughts

Vote target : 50 votes

I won't update until it's completed like I did for this chapter

Angel...

8. I was a virgin too..

R^{YAN}

Fuck. My head hurts, the first thing I registered after opening my eyes along with a light weight of something on my chest.

I looked down to see a brunette hair of someone laying down on me with my arms around her, when I looked closely I realised who it was,

DISHA

Fuck when did we end up like this, that's when I noticed under the sheer velvet blanket we both were naked, what the fuck has happened here

I felt her stirring in her sleep, I just hope she wakes up so we can talk

After few minutes of stirring, her eyes flutter open and she blinks few times before adjusting to the light, and soon meeting my eyes, with blush tinting her cheeks

God why is she blushing her cheeks is now pink just like her lips, my eyes trailed down her lips, it was so full and plump, god I just want to kis-

Just stop it, Ryan don't act like a fucking teenager, don't forget why this girl is here as your fucking wife

"What happened yesterday" I asked, already regretting drinking 5 glass of vodka

"Umm you don't remember" her blushing intensified even more

"I wouldn't have asked then now would I" I said, my tone harsh because I noticed her flinching visibly, I don't care I just need the damn answer even though I have a rough idea where this would lead but still I wanted to be sure

"Umm you know.. we did that.. that couples do" she said stuttering

She couldn't even say we had sex or just fucked each other because no way in hell I will make love to that women

"And you let me fuck you even though I was clearly drunk you took advantage of my drunkenness because you knew very well there is no way in hell I will ever touch you let alone fuck you, TELL ME" I shouted and by now she had tears in her eyes

"I... tried to stop you" she said while hiccuping

"Oh so now you are pushing all this on me when I was probably not even in my senses, wow disha you are an wonderful actor" saying this I went into the washroom, not caring I was butt naked

As soon as I shut the door I could hear her sobs and cries, to be honest it did something to me I just couldn't understand what it did to me but it probably didn't made me happy

Shut up Ryan don't be a fool, don't forget whose daughter she is and why is she here

I somewhat feel angry at myself how can I sleep with her even if I was drunk, I can't believe she was my first I gave my virginity to her gosh but somewhere in my heart I also feel happy, just don't know why

Heart matters are stupid so it's better if we shut it

Coming out of the shower, I knew she was still curled up in the blanket, I went into my closet without sparing her a glance, harsh I know but this is how I am

By the time I came out she was already inside the bathroom and the clothes that were scattered all around were no where in sight

I sighed in relief, didn't needed a reminder of what happened yesterday

As I was spraying my cologne, she came out of the bathroom with just her towel around her, I just don't know if she was always like this or things change once you have sex, cause right now she looked what you could say is...sexy

With water droplets dropping from her hair till disappearing inside her towel, I am definitely not developing a boner righ now do I, oh god this is embarassing, this is all her fault if she didn't had sex with me then I wouldn't had found her this.. appealing...

Don't lie you horny bastard you always have and always will find her appealing, don't forget you always used to glance at her secretly when you thought no one was looking.. my subconscious mocked me

By the time my eyes landed where she was standing a few minutes back she was already there fully clothed and ready.

Ignoring her like I always do, I took my briefcase I exited my room and went downstairs

"Good morning everyone" I greeted everyone with a small fake smile

After sometime she came down too and sat on her usual seat which is across me and besides kritika

Soon the breakfast were served by the maids and everyone started munching on their breakfast

Then somebody cleared their throat, I looked up from my plate to see it was dadi who did it

"As everyone knows I have not been here in my grandson's marriage but that doesn't mean I won't give him and his newlywedded wife any gift, Rajesh ji please bring it" One of our servants bought something in an envelope

I understood right away what it is, tickets she gifted me and raghav too

I just hated it not the place but to go with her as a couple

"I have booked your ticket to Paris I hope you enjoy it" Dadi said and samaira started coughing loudly

"Me and him? Together" she asked

"Yes samaira do you have any problem" dadi said and God she can be threatening at times when needed

After that everything went peacefully and I went to my office Rudra not joining me today cause his flight for Paris is booked for tonight so he can't come with me to office today

Sitting in car, I seriously pressured my brain to remember what happened yesterday

Flashes started passing my eyes, slowly and steadily I started remembering everything, looks like what she said was true I was the one insisting but still I was drunk and she was sober

I still don't know why I drank that much, was it because I was angry, but why, yeah I felt a little jealous a tiny part of me felt it, because she mentioned I was not her first love but can it really be true???

Was I really jealous??

#######

How was the chapter??

Thoughts about Ryan??

So I have decided few things I will let you all know...

i. Updates of this book would be just on Wednesday. So please don't spam before that.

ii. As you all don't care about vote target there would be none

iii. From now on I won't show any ones particular pov, it would be third person pov and I will try to show all three couples in all chapters

That's it

Signing off-

9. Doubts of insecurities?

THIRDPERSON

I shouldn't have done it knowing very well what would be the outcome, how dumb can I be , Disha thought to herself

She knew that her husband didn't love her and her love would always remain one-sided, and she would lie to herself if she says it didn't pinch her heart everytime she thought about it

She knew what done was done, she gave away her virginity due to her naive thinking that it would change anything and it led to her only in her pool of regrets

What is done is done, she thought to herself and went inside the chemist store, and straightaway towards the section where that activity related things are kept

She quickly took what needed, a birth control pill, she took enough of blame on herself and she didn't want her husband to loathe her even more, like he doesn't loathe her now

But moreover she didn't wanted to conceive a child when spending night with her holded no meaning for her husband

She wants children but not like this, she wanted it to born out of love not out of guilt and regret

As soon as she sat down in her car and the driver started driving and headed towards the mansion

She took out her bottle which is always kept in her bag and quickly gulped down the pill with water

After keeping everything in the bag, her mind again wandered off to the morning incident

Unwillingly, tears pooled in her eyes, he said she has taken advantage of him, she tried to stop him many times didn't she then how is it her fault..

But in her mind she already blamed herself, only if she hadn't let her harmones take control of her she wouldn't have regreted so much in the morning

######

Here, Samaira was already dreading her honeymoon

Gosh I just hope he doesn't murder me there, she thought

"We have a flight in few hours or do you still wanna stay and beautify your ugly face" she didn't want to admit it but her harsh words really felt like a needle pearcing in her tiny heart

She never viewed herself ugly or less beautiful because for her her outside doesn't matter, but people around her always seems to remind her that

"Oh hello I am talking to you" the demon's voice bought her out of reverie

Without saying anything she joined her outside in the bedroom, she was in her closet gathering all the courage she had to go on a honeymoon with the dickhead she calls her husband

He was typing something away on his phone, she cleared her throat to gain his attention

He looked up from his phone and roamed his eyes on her, she felt naked even after so many layers of clothes, just because his eyes were grazing at her intensely

"For this you took 2 fucking hours" his tone matching the look on his face, disgust

'I thought he would atleast give me a compliment after he watched me like that' she thought

"Let's go I don't have any more time to waste"

With that she followed her around like a lost puppy, she hated that type of a feeling

Upon reaching downstairs she had to meet everyone and bid her goodbye

"Raghuvanshi's daughter in law dressed like that" her mother in law's voice boomed in the living room and it irritated the shit out of her

"I don't think anyone goes to Paris wearing saree now do they?" Samaira replied and she could see how her other two bhabhis were trying to control their laugh and her mother in law fuming in anger

"Enough of this let's go" Okay now he sounded straightaway pissed and she thought it's best to obey him

And with that they sat in their car which would take them to the airport, even the airport is owned by the Raghuvanshi's

As the airport is at a distance she sighed and laid back closing her eyes

#####

After completing the chores, kritika like always came inside his bedroom

Just to see him already sitting on the bed, isn't he at the gym at this hour

Yeah everyone does it in the morning but this husband of hers do it in night

Ignoring him and the fact he should be in gym now she went to change her clothes, this one was really sticky with all the sweat

She opened her walk in closet and took out her pyjamas for the night

I just love satin, and at night it's a whole different story, she thought

She was about to remove my kurti, when she heard him clearing his throat behind her

Placing her kurti back in place, she cautiously turned around to see if he was really standing there

Heart,now is not the time to beat so fast and jump out of my ribcage, he is just standing there

"Listen kritika about what happened few days back at par-" and her full anger surfaced back

"No raghav it's okay if you have came here to apologise then no need to do that because at that time I saw it myself that you can trust someone like your investors son with whom you don't even have a relationship but trusting your wife is too much to ask isn't it, so that's why I don't even asked for explanation and no need to give it too" She said and finally she let go of what she considered a burden on her chest

It was just too hard to keep it all inside, those words, those feelings, feeling of unwanted, feeling of uneasiness it was just too much for her

After that she didn't know what happened in a second he moved infront of her and eventually pinned her on the nearest wall with both her hand beside her head and his fingers interlocked with hers

His full body pressed on her, chest to chest, he basically outlined her body

But this time she didn't backed out, this time even she looked daringly in his eyes, his beautiful brown eyes which had specks of grey in it

She didn't knew how but his eyes always mesmerized her actually everything about him is mesmerizing, in comparison to him she was a plain jane with chestnut brown hair and brown eyes matching it

She won't call herself curvy but not skinny either she was somewhere in middle

I don't have anything specific in my body which someone would fall in love, maybe that's the reason my own husband can never love me, she thought

######

Double update... Yahoo!!

Tell your thoughts about the chapter...

Next chapter I will try to give more insights on the other two guys

So did you liked the third person pov or should I continue first person

Next update on Wednesday...

Signing off..

Angel

10. Sorry?

K RITIKA

He was standing really close now, we were practically breathing the same air now, but now I refuse to back out, he was the wrong one here

"What are you doing raghav" I croaked out

"I want you to listen to me and you will

I am sorry for that day and i shouldn't have reacted the way I did"

"Over, or do you want to say something else, if it's done then please leave me" I said calmly

He looked shock, haha as if he would give a little speech of apology and I would accept it like nothing happened

But he left me like I asked too and I turned around, my back facing him

I turned my head a little and said, "You can leave now please"

With that he left, leaving me with my thoughts

His touches do effect me in a way but that doesn't mean I will melt in pool of muddle and let him go away with that incident so easily

I did what I came to do here, changing into my nightwear and went outside

Seeing the time, it was only 9, not wanting to sleep so early, I started looking for the tv remote, yeah everyone has their personal tv in their rooms

Where the fucking hell is the tv remote? I left it on the bed only last time..

Not wanting to talk to him I started searching everywhere, I could even feel his gaze following me

I then searched in the last remaining place, the drawers, I bent down to search for it, I could still feel his gaze on me, more particularly my ass which was in air

Ignoring it, I resumed my searching, and yes! Found it!

Taking the remote, I turned on the tv while sitting on the bed and covering myself fully with duvet, this pervert is really getting on my nerves

Ignoring him I switched to Netflix, I love watching Korean dramas on it

I quickly switched on my one of my fav drama of all time my girl

I am in love with their main leads, it's my fourth time watching it

.....

By the time I reached 4 episode I noticed he was also watching, with quite interest I might add

"Liking the show" I asked and he actually got startled

"Yeah it a nice show" he replied and I nodded

"Can't believe he is spending millions just to develop a foundation" he said

"He is feeling guilty, guilt can make you do greater things" I replied and then turned off the tv, it's time to sleep now for me

I turned off the lights too and my bedside lamp too, soon I was drifting away in my sleep until I heard him saying,

"Indeed guilt can make you making great things but love can make you do even greater things"

######

DISHA

I kept on turning and tossing in my sleep, but sleep was faraway from away from me, maybe it's the fact that he is sitting right here but I couldn't gather the courage to say what I want too

But you should say it after all it's your mistake, with my inner thought I took a deep breath and sat upright against my headboard and turned on my bedside lamp..

Before I could say anything, I could already feel his eyes on me

I cleared my throat and I started my thoughts before my every ounce of courage disappears

"Ryan, about what happened last night I am sorry, you are right I shouldn't have overstepped my boundaries, you were drunk and I was sober but still I let my irrational thinking took over and all of that happened

And I am really very sorry for that, I know that what I did is practically taking advantage of you and if the roles were reversed here my outburst would have been more severe than you and I know one sorry can never make anything right.. but I do hope you forgive me" Saying this all in one breath, I finally stopped

After saying everything, I got up from my bed, and started walking towards the door

"Where are you going?"

"To one of the guest room, I think after what happened I think it's best if we stay away from each other" with that I left the room and started walking towards the guest room which I already prepared in the afternoon...

I felt a huge weight lifted off my chest after the apology and with that I laid down on my bed, darkness consuming me..

######

S A M A I R A

When I opened my eyes again I was sleeping in a bedroom, What the fricking hell?? We reached Paris so soon

"No we are still in my private jet" I got startled by voice that came from beside me

"You jerk you scared me" I turned to look at him and he again had his glasses on and working on his laptop

"I guess I am supposed to say sorry or what" he said, his tone bored

"Yes, but I think a idiot like you won't know it"

"who do you called a idiot, for your information I am a Harvard graduate but a middle class girl like you can never understand it" He really hitted the right nerve, I may be poor and middle class but I was happy with what I have

"Alas you have a Harvard degree but you lack one thing which no University in this whole universe can give a human, MANNERS, and i think this MIDDLE CLASS GIRL has more manners than you, A HARVARD

GRADUATE" I emphasized each word and I went outside the room of the private jet and sat down on one of the couches...

No wonder he is a rich spoiled brat, I think he is a total male version of his mother, I wonder if their father was like this too??

Shut up samaira what are you saying, don't bring a dead man into all this, let him rest in peace, I scolded myself

Why drag him because of that jerk and his mother, I can't believe I am alone in a plane with him, when we were in India atleast he can't do any harm to me, but now he can practically murder me and no one would even know...

Thank God I bought all type of safety things with me..

Pepper spray, a knife and few more things, atleast I would be safe from that jerk

With that thought I sighed and leaned back in my seat, enjoying the view outside..

#####

So yes guys I updated, but for a reason

I am going on a vacation from 25 of Feb till 5 of March and I can't update in between but I would update till 25 as many chapters I can

Hope you enjoyed today's chapter!!

Comment and vote

Signing off -

Angel

11. Bathing and Falling

SAMAIRA

Finally we have landed in the city of love and I must admit it's beautiful out here, I looked beside me to see he was still busy in his phone typing away something furiously

"I know I am breathe-takingly handsome but no need to stare like a creep" his voice made me blush deep red, embarassed for getting caught red handed, I was indeed checking him out

"Haha as if keep dreaming" I said and turned to see the view outside

The car came to sudden hault, and he was already out of car, he have a speed of fricking vampire

I stepped out of the car and came in view with a beautiful mansion, drop dead beautiful it was magnificent

"Are planning to stay outside because clearly I will be certainly pleased by it" he voice broke my beautiful trance, stupid man

I hurriedly followed him inside, and I looked everywhere in awe, inside was even more beautiful

"Don't gawk like an idiot" god his voice is so irritating

"I am sorry if looking at new things and appreciating makes me idiot" I replied, sarcasm dripping from my nerves, and it seem it hitted a nerve

"You-" "Welcome back Ansh you are back after such a long time" he was cut short by a lady around his mom's age

"Mariah you still here?" "Of course I am after all I am the care taker of this house and may I ask who this beautiful lady is" she asked facing me with a gentle smile on her face

He snorted like her calling me beautiful was funny and I quickly glared at him, and introduced myself, "Hello aunty I am Samaira"

"Samaira as in Ansh's wife, so nice to meet you finally dadi told me about you" I just smiled in response

"I have prepared food for two people and I am sorry to say but I can't come tomorrow as I am grandmother of two, I have to take care of them, if you can handle everything then it's okay but if not I can send someone"

"It's okay we can handle" He said and I looked at him shocked

With that Mariah aunty left and he turned towards me with his stupid smirk on his face

He suddenly started walking towards me but instead of feeling intimated by him and moving back, like I read in those stupid novels, I stood my ground and looked at him staring in his honey coloured eyes

He was now really close, our noses were touching and we were breathing the same air

"Don't you feel scared, Mrs Raghuvanshi we are both alone here and the fact I can practically do anything to you" Smugness can be sensed from his tone

I looked into his eyes and answered, "What more can you do? You have already ruined my life by marrying me? What else you can do, murder me or tie me and starve me to death, huh tell me Mr Raghuvanshi" I said in a mocking tone

Looks like he has never be challenged, as soon as said that his eyes literally went shades darker

Sensing in what position in we are I just took a step back and said, "I would appreciate it if you don't evade my personal space because I very much like it"

"Now I would like to know where is my room" I know for a fact if his family is not here he will not stay in one room as me

"In the East wing is your room and mine would be west side" saying this he went away and I started walking towards my room

------

As my clothes and other things were already settled down in my closet, it didn't took much time for me to settle down, I took the bath and right now I am sitting in the dining room, waiting for him

"Ahhh" I heard a loud scream and I think I went deaf for a second, it's his voice

Oh my god what happened to him, I hurriedly started running towards his room, upon reaching there he was no where in sight, again I heard a scream and it came from bathroom

My mind was screaming at me to not go in and let him be in pain but I just couldn't do that now can I, I entered the bathroom with my back facing inside, I certainly don't want to see him naked

"What happened why are you screaming" I asked, not liking how concerned I am for this douche

"What are you doing here" wow, being the nice person I am I came to help him and this person, unbelievable

"Okay if you don't wanna tell then I will go" as I started walking out, he called out

"Wait, I think I sprained my ankle, come here near the tub so I can get up"

"I think something is missing from your sentence" I said smirking, not that he can see it

"What" he certainly sounded angry

"The word 'please' is missing, say it and I might help you" I said smiling like crazy, I won't let this chance go away so easily

The great Rudransh Raghuvanshi was asking for my help, how can I let it go away

"I think you have lost your mind I won't do anything that you are asking for"

"Okay then goodluck on getting up on your own" I said and started walking out

"Okay, I will do it, samaira please help me get out of the tub"

"Now that wasn't so difficult was it" saying this I started backwards till my legs touched the bathtub

"Keep your hands on my shoulder and get up" I said and bent down a little so he could grab my shoulder

As he was getting up, due to the water he again slipped and fell into the tub, splashing water outside the tub too, some fell near my legs

"Give me your hand" he said and complied quickly

He was getting up but he again slipped this time, but he just didn't slipped alone he also took me in the tub

"Ahh" a scream escaped my lips

"What the hell Rudransh you can't even get up, you even pulled me into the tub and got me all wet" I screamed but then I noticed his eyes were somewhere else

I trailed down where his eyes were, and my eyes widened, I was wearing a fricking white shirt and because of getting wet my whole bra's outline is showing

I quickly got up from the tub and took the robe from the cabinet and put it on and started going outside

"Hey where are you going who is going to help me" he shouted but I was in no mood to listen that pervert was literally staring at my chest

I was not a devil to leave him like that so I told Sam, our driver to help him getting out of the bathroom and I went in my room to take care of my wet clothes

This time I took out nude colour undergarments with black top on it to wear and black sweatpants

It's better to be safe than sorry

######

As I felt that our samaira and rudra weren't getting much importance here is the whole chapter on them

Do vote and comment..

So guys I wanted to make a playlist on Spotify for this book so if you all have any song suggestions then please do give them, but it should relate and give this book's vibe

Suggest the songs here --------->

Signing off -

Angel

12. A Meet Of Past

DISHA

"Hello, Sara I am coming to the supermarket and I have sent you the list please keep that things read I will come and pick it up" saying this I ended the call

I wonder how things can get over so fast in this house, but then again almost 10 people live here

Even though the Raghuvanshi's are so rich it's the daughter in law's job to bring every necessities in to the house, I mean how stupid one could be

I just took my phone and left the mansion, no need for money, perks of owning the supermarket

I instructed the driver to take me to the the supermarket and soon the journey started

After some time the car haulted and I got down and made my way towards the supermarket

Taking the things from Sara I started making my way towards the exit but just then my body bumped into someone's chest and everything fell from my hand on to the floor

"I am so sor-" my words got stuck in my throat when I saw with whom I bumped..

"Harsh"

#####

R Y A N

"You better have a fucking reason to call me Sameer otherwise forgot you even had a job" I barked, I have so much work pending and these idiots keep disturbing me

"Sir you told me to go wherever disha mam goes so today we came to super-market but then she met someone and gave me the groceries and everything and went away with her friend" he said, I could feel him trembling from here, what can I do people are fucking scared from me

"So, now I also have to keep track of her friends or what"

"Sir actually her friend is a man and she was actually laughing and smiling with him" now this actually got my attention

"Where are they now?" I asked with a hint of anger

"The went to the nearby Starbucks" he said and I ended the call with only one thing in my mind..

Who was he??

I clenched my hands tightly after seeing the sight infront of me, that harsh or whoever he was touching her hand, both sitting in a cafe right now

Calm down Ryan eventually you are going to leave her, she can be with whoever she want, but right now she is still my wife..

And for this you definitely have to give answers Mrs Raghuvanshi

I won't let this slide so easily..

With that I ordered my driver to drive back to the company

#####

DISHA

"Harsh you here?" I say with a glint of happiness

"Disha, my god you have turned even more beautiful than before" he said and I blushed slightly due to that

We both walked towards the exit and once I reached towards the car I instructed the driver to take the groceries home, I will come in sometime

Turning back I bumped into his chest and out of instinct I moved back a little but my clumsy self just tripped on my own legs and he quickly saved me by holding my hips

"I see still your clumsy old self" he joked after steadying me on my legs

"Yeah nothing changed much" except me getting married and falling crazily in one sided love for my husband

"So should we go to the cafe for some catching up" he said and ofcourse I said yes

And here we are sitting in the cafe, talking about something past, something about present

"So do you have a girlfriend?" I asked out of blue

"Why still trying to get with me?" He joked and I snorted

"As if" it didn't felt like he was ex boyfriend, it felt like we were bestfriend

"But really disha I was hoping we can work on our relationship" saying this he took my hand in his

I didn't what happened but this gesture didn't felt right, he is my ex boyfriend and I have a husband now

Retreating my hand back, I drank my coffee and continued, "Harsh I think it's too late for that, I am already married to someone else"

"I understand but we can always remain friends isn't it, I think I don't have your number in my new phone give it to me now" he said passing me his phone and I quickly saved my number in it under my name

"Here" I said passing it back to him, my eyes wandered back to my watch and my eyes widened, I need to go

"Harsh I really loved meeting you but now I have to go" Saying this I started leaving when he stopped me, "Don't forget to call me let's meet again sometime" he suggested and I nodded

"For sure I will contact you" "I can drop you if you want" I agreed because it's late right now and I don't want to walk

We both say in his car and he started driving with me giving him the directions

"You can stop here" I said stopping him few metres away from the mansion, reason I don't want anyone to see him, especially my witch of a mother in law

"Are you sure?" I nodded and got down from the car and waved my hand at him to say goodbye

"Bye. Go safely" saying this I took of to the mansion

I entered my bedroom in which I have shifted, and as soon as my gaze landed on the bed my breathe got stuck in my throat

Ryan was sitting on the bed, his eyes were red - bloodshot red, and this whole room stinks with him being the source of the whole odour

I assume he has drunk again, god not again, I am not fully over what happened last time when he was drunk I don't want another episode of it

"Where were you?"

"Huh"

"I asked where were you" his voice raised a little

"I was out with a friend"

"A friend or lover" he asked sarcastically and my eyes bulged out at his statement

######

So how was it????

Thoughts about Ryan and disha??

One more thing I have updated a playlist of this book in the 'intro' chapter, do check it out

You can still suggest some songs and I will surely add it in the playlist

Signing off -

Angel

13. Talks...

D ISHA

"What do you mean?" I asked, shocked

"Oh so now playing innocent and unknown" he said, tauntingly

"Ryan if you want to say something say clearly otherwise please leave my room you are clearly drunk and I am not in the mood to do anything right now" I said with a sigh

"So who was he with you in the cafe" he asked and then it clicked he was talking about Harsh

"How do you know I was in the cafe, were you stalking me?" I gasped at the realisation

"So it is true you were indeed in the cafe with your lover" he said with a scowl

And this ticked off my anger, this man really has the audacity to say and behave like this when he told me he doesn't care about me, "yeah I was with my lover in that cafe and not just anyone but with my first love, Harsh and guess what I was very happy after meeting him and as for you, you don't hold any right on me so you can't ask me any questions about my personal life" I finished fuming in anger

"And I don't understand why are you here after all the type of relationship we have is not one of the greatest so please leave" with that I went to the washroom to take a bath, after few minutes I even heard the door clicking and I sighed in relief

Finally he left..

After 30 minutes I came out of the bath and wrapped a towel around me and came out of the bathroom, my breathe got stuck in my throat for the second time in the night

Here I thought he left but he was still there sitting on my bed like a king, "I think I told you to leave" I said irritated

"And do you really think I take orders?" He turned towards me and his eyes roaming all over me

Suddenly I became self conscious, I was just in a damn towel

I went towards my closet and quickly took my clothes for the night and turned around just to bump in his hard chest

I gasped backing up against the closet due to our closeness, "wha..tt are you doing" I mentally slapped myself for stuttering

"Why isn't it's a husband right to be close to his wife"

"No wife's consent also matters we wifes are not just some damn property so please move back"

"Why are you resisting isn't this what you wanted just like last time when you slept with me" and that's it now this man has just crossed his line

"Oh really I was the one who slept with you or you were the one who was insisting to sleep with me

I gave myself to you, made you my first because I love you but next day I came to my senses after hearing your words and I knew the moment we shared that night, for me it was a moment of love but for you it was just your sexual frustration, just because you were drunk and I apologised dosen't mean you weren't at fault at all" I finished and by that time it was me who has backed him up till the door

I leaned in him we were so close that our noses were almost kissing each other and he stood still there..

'Click'..

I opened the door behind him and pushed him outside and quickly locked the door..It all happened so quickly he didn't even had time to react

Soon banging can be heard on my door but I don't give a damn let him break his hand

I wore my clothes and jumped on the bed with the duvet over me and sleep coaxing me in its arms

######

KRITIKA

"Ahh it feels so calm here, so peaceful" I mumbled to myself, soft winds hitting my face

Right now I am standing in the balcony it's the most peaceful corner in this room

"I see enjoying the view" a voice boomed behind me and startled I turned around

"Why do you always have to scare me" I said and again faced the beautiful sky

"Umm habit I think" I don't know why but I feel he is speaking to me now more than he spoke ever in past 6 months of our marriage, not that I am complaining

"I think someday this habit of yours will surely kill me with a heartattack" I replied

"So what are you doing here all alone"

"It's just peaceful here so I try to spend more time here" I replied and he hummed

"So what are you doing here" I asked

"Actually I wanted you to find me a file I can't find it anywhere" he spoke and I stood straight

"Which file?" And then he told me which one and I went into the closet to find it, I kept all his file there only

He told me he wanted his work file and it was blue colour

Soon enough I found it as I was removing it another paper fell infront of me and just down at my feet

I picked it up and was about to keep it back in his place when a certain word caught my attention and the world slipped beneath my feet

The papers fell from my hand and tears pooled in my eyes and only one thing roaming in my head

'DIVORCE'

######

Haha yes your author is evil, not wanted to end the chapter on cliffhanger but the next chapter would be out tomorrow

I can't believe I am writing chapters back to back

Do vote and comment your thoughts

Signing off -

Angel

14. Incident in Library..

KRITIKA

Why is there divorce papers in his closet, I picked the paper again and it confirmed my fears

It was made on the exact date, the same day we got married, means he wanted to get rid of one day

Tears unwantedly started flowing from my eyes until a knock bought me in reality

"Hello have you slept in there or what?" His voice held a bit of playfulness

I quickly wiped my eyes and stuffed the papers back and took the file he wanted and stood up quickly

Don't be silly Kritika, if he wanted a divorce he would have taken long back, you are married to him don't think like this

Saying and encouraging myself I came outside of the closet and handed him the file, trying the push the previous memories faraway in my mind

"Why are you so pale?" He asked and I chewed my lips, contemplating what to tell him, I certainly can't tell him I literally found a divorce papers in his closet now can I?

"Nothing I will go to sleep now" saying this I went to my side of the bed and quickly covered myself with the duvet, trying to sleep....

I just hope whatever I saw in the closet isn't the truth and I really don't get away from him, call me idiot for wanting to stay in such a marriage but I just don't care, my heart wants him and just him...

I just hope everything will be fine.. with a sigh I let sleep finally overtake my senses...

#####

RAGHAV

"Brother, is it really necessary to do all this" raghav asked, if anyone in the trio is considered less ruthless then it's him

His brothers always topped in ruthlessness

"Don't forget raghav our family is today here because of them" Ryan said

"But it isn't their fault now is it why are we punishing them"

"It wasn't our mom's fault either but even she payed for the price and don't forget everyone has to price for what their loved one do"

Rustling of papers bought me back to my reality, with me sitting in my home office

I checked the wall clock and it indicated 2pm now, but still sleep faraway from my eyes

I stood up and went towards the bar area and took out a whiskey, as soon as the glass touched my lips I stopped, I kept it back and started walking away from it

When my brothers made this plan which involved innocents in it, I was hesitant first but then I did background research on her and I am glad now I agreed on it

If it wasn't for her then my chipmunk would have been with me, she wouldn't have died but she is not and it's all her fault

I HATE YOU KRITIKA

######

S A M A I R A

God, it's so boring sitting idle all alone in this bigass house, good thing it has huge and lavish library

I can't believe I am here for honeymoon, I am sitting here in the library and he is enjoying himself out there

Shaking all that thoughts out, I brought my concentration on the book, a erotica I am reading right now, yeah I am into smut so what

"Didn't knew you were into kinky things" A voice spoke behind me, startled I dropped my book

"What the hell Rudransh" I squeaked

"Well I just came back from a meeting and Maria told me you are here and when I checked on you, I saw my wife was reading a smut book" he said, his usual smirk on his face, and if you are wondering then yes he works even here

"So what if I am reading a smut book or anything for that it shouldn't concern you" I huffed angrily and bent to pick up the book

As soon as I turned back to him, I regretted it he was so close to me I could smell his cologne, god times like this I regretted being short heighted, I only reached till his chest and I had to strain my neck to look him in the eyes

"What the hell are you doing?" I shrieked

"Well what's the fun in reading it, why not we try some of that in real life" he said smugly, and me on the other hand flushed red because of his unfiltered words.

"What are you saying and get aside" I tried to move him but this giant of a man didn't moved a inch

"What say should I show you a demo right now" my breathe hitched, his hand started roaming on hips and going dangerously low, and this bastard was smirking

I was turning the wheels in brain to get out of this and then it struck me, if he wanted to play like this then so it be

I roamed my hands on his chest and everything wouldn't have been so calm in the room I would have missed his groan, reaching for his collar I pulled him down so that my lips are just beside his ears, breathing near him I whispered

"I would love it..." I took long pause and then continued

"But too bad not from a jerk like you" saying this I pushed him away with all my strength, and since he was distracted it was a lot more easier

Taking my book I started walking towards the door of library, when he said

"Do you really think I would touch a girl like for real??" I could hear disgust in his tone

I turned around, "well you just did if not you then you little friend over there certainly did" I gestured towards his pants and it was certainly having a hard time

"And good luck with that and make sure not to be too loud" I said smirking and with that I went away

######

So how was it?? Thoughts??

Isn't samaira just evil?? Perfect match for Rudransh *smirk*

Thoughts about kritika and raghav??

Don't forget to vote..

Signing off -

Angel

15. Meetings...

D^{ISHA}

Past few days have been wonderful, I can't believe meeting harsh would be so wonderful, it's like a little colour in my dull life

Right now I am getting ready to meet him we are going to the fair that he recommended us few days back

This time I decided to ditch my usual Indian attire and go with something modern and western, thank god my mother in law has left along with dadi and saanvi as she has to attend her last year of college

After wearing my outfit, i styled my hair and wore my gold accessories that go with the outfit and styled it with a sling bag and the only pair of heels I own, applying minimal amount of makeup and tada I am ready to go

My phone's ringtone was suddenly heard in the bedroom and I skipped over the room to find it, once I found it I pressed on the answer without even seeing who was calling

"Harsh I-" "Disha" hearing the voice my own voice died in my throat, I looked down and it was Ryan, god disha how stupid you can be

Keeping the phone near my ear I asked, "what happened why did you called me"

"I have left a file at home bring it to my office now" "but can't Manish bring the file I have to be somewhere" I protested, but the reason is I don't wanna face him after what happened last we haven't even talked after that

"You can go to your lover after you deliver the file, this file is important for today's meeting, bring it immediately because if you be late then consequences would be severe" saying this the line went dead

I cursed expletives at him and then I calmed myself, relax disha just give him the file and get away from there

Saying and encouraging myself I searched for the file he want and took a look at myself for the last time and started walking out

As I reached the kitchen I stopped to inform kritika, "kritika Ryan needs a file so I am dropping this at his office and then going out with my friend"

"Okay bhabhi and by the way you look great" she said with that I exited the house

Sitting in one of the expensive car owned by Ryan, I told the driver to take me to the destination, Raghuvanshi inc...

It was full 30 minutes ride from the mansion and I am glad we finally reached, I took a deep breath just give him this file and leave

I stepped out and closed the door with a light thud, being one of the wealthiest man wife can be little challenging, keeping my back straight and chin high, I started taking long and confident strides

In a matter of minutes, I was infront of the elevator, I could hear the employees whisper

'Isn't it disha mam?'

'They make such a cute couple'

'her dress is so good'

These were some things I heard before I entered the personal elevator only for Raghuvanshi family and friends

These people only know what we show, if they would know what we are in real life they wouldn't think us as ideal couple

I pressed 90th button, yeah this building is fricking huge, the elevator stopped with a ding and I stepped out of it and went straight for his cabin

His secratary greeted me on the way and I greeted her back, okay now is the real deal, should I knock on the door first or directly enter inside

Okay even if he is my husband I shouldn't forget my manners, let's knock first and with that I knocked on his door, "Come in" he ordered his voice gruff

I entered the door and walked near his desk and kept the file on his desk, "Your file"

He looked up from his laptop and his eyes felt like he was scanning me from head to toe

"I see fully ready to meet your lover, huh" him and his sarcasm, I just rolled my eyes, "yep have to look good" I said with a sweet smile

I started leaving when he again stopped me, "Did I told you to leave" "last time I checked I didn't had to take anyone's permission for anything, so goodbye you wanted your file and I bought now I will get going"

"Be sure to not do anything which would tarnish my family's name" he said arrogantly

"I have never did anything in my one year of marriage life so I know I won't do something now or in future too" saying I left

Why can't these men mind their business and shut up for once, but no if they do that then their ego will surely get bruised

Pushing this thoughts away I quickly sent a message to harsh that I am arriving soon

#####

KRITIKA

No one is in the house right now and now is the right time to take a dip in the pool, with that thought I changed into my two piece swimsuit, the only sexy piece of clothing I own in my entire wordrobe, another thing of being the raghuvanshi's daughter in law, always dress modest not even slightly revealing clothes

I put on my robe over it, not want the maids gwaking at me

I hurriedly walked towards the pool room, yeah we had it inside the mansion, I closed the door behind me and slipped off my robe

The room had music system installed to it so you just have to connect your Bluetooth and you are all set to play your music and that's what I did, I connected my phone and started playing one of my favourite of all time

Harleys in Hawaii by Katy pery

I jumped into the pool right after that, it's damn refreshing to be in pool like this, I started swaying my hips in the pool with the beats of music

I'll be your baby, on a Sunday

Oh, why don't we get out of town?

Call me your baby, on the same wave

Oh, no, no, there's no slowin' down

You and I, I

Ridin' Harleys in Hawaii-i-i

I'm on the back, I'm holdin' tight, I

Want you to take me for a ride, ride

When I hula-hula, hula

So good, you'll take me to the jeweler-jeweler, jeweler

There's pink and purple in the sky-y-y

We're ridin' Harleys in Hawaii-i-i

I sang along with the lyrics, I have literally memorized it I love this song

"I didn't knew a karaoke is going in our pool" I followed the source of voice and there he was standing with his arms folded at his chest

"Good thing I don't charge money for my singing" I said back

"Oh trust me no one wants to hear your croaked voice my ear would have bled if you continued singing one more minute" he said and I glared at him

Thinking now it's enough of swimming I swam back to the stairs of the pool and started climbing back up, I could feel his eyes on me

"No need to stare with such intensity I can literally feel you boring hole in my back" I said while wrapping my robe around me

"And who said I was doing it I was in a deep thought and not staring at you"

"Whatever helps you sleep at night" I retorted

"Alexa please turn on the heater" I say because I was literally shivering with cold

"You shouldn't be in the pool if you can't handle the cold" he said while sitting beside me on the bench

"Who said I am cold I am perfectly fine" I said denying even though it was true my teeths were chattering again each other

"You should practice lying then probably you would be able to lie properly.. come here" he said opening his jacket button and I shook me head stubbornly

"No it's okay" I said

Then abruptly he took a hold of my forearm and pulled me against his chest with his jacket around both of us

I tried to move but he kept his hands tight around me, I don't know what is happening on one side he is keeping me warm and on the other side I have found divorce papers in his closet, Mt mind is functioning properly after this, I sighed and kept laying on his chest, savouring the moment as long as it can last...

######

SAMAIRA

"Rudransh either take me out somewhere or else take me back to India I can't be here locked in this house anymore" I said barging in his room, enough is enough I am fucking bored in this bigass house

"Didn't I told you to not enter my room" he glared at me

"And didn't you listened what I just told you" I glared at him with the same intensity

"You are not a fucking baby and I am not your baby sitter so leave you are a grown up woman for godsakes I don't think you need me to take you somewhere"

"You are right why would I need you and just remember one thing Rudransh Raghuvanshi if I got lost in this place na then it all will be your fault" saying this I left, closing the door with a loud bang

######

So guys how was it??

Thoughts on Disha and Ryan??

What about Kritika and Raghav??

Samaira is really something else isn't it?? And what about Rudransh??

Samaira and Rudransh part would be continued in next chapter

Signing off -

Angel

16. Walk and Talks

I got dressed in one of favourite sweater and skirt and paired it with some gold accessories to go with it

If that dumb creature doesn't want to go anywhere with me then it's okay I will go outside and enjoy myself

I took my sling bag and kept my phone in it along with some stack of cash

"Okay all set now let's rock n roll" I said out to no one in particular

I opened Google maps on my phone and started my journey to one of the most expensive mall in here

It was at a 30 minutes distance from his mansion and after a little tiring walk I reached my destination

I entered Victoria's secret shop to buy something for myself I have heard great things about this shop let's try it today

I went into the lingeries section and started searching for anything that I would like

A certain lace black colour lingerie caught my eyes

I took a look at its price and my eyes bulged out of its socket, 600$ Nearly 45,000 in Indian rupees

Too expensive, I kept it back in its place and exited the shop, have you gone mad samaira clearly that shop is more expensive than your monthly expenses

I decided to rome a little more in the city and explore it's beauty, but soon that little walk turned into a 2 hour walk and I forgot the way back to the mansion

"Shit" I cursed as I noticed my phone has been switched off due to low battery

Deciding I can't stay sitting here in the park I got up and started walking to a direction I think I came from

Walking for few minutes I understood I am just walking into nowhere

"Hey hotcake" I heard a wolf whistle from behind me and I turned around me to see 3 guys standing there or more like stumbling here and there

Clearly they are drunk and I have no buisness with them so ignoring them I started my walk again, my pace a little hurried than last time

I can clearly hear them following me and that's when I took up my speed but obviously they are three and I am just alone so they catched up with me

The surrounded me when one of them said, "not so fast shortcake" and then I knew shit would happen....

######

RUDRANSH

"God where have this girl gone" I groaned while calling her for the 10th time in the night

It's 11pm now and she is no where in sight, I didn't knew she will really go to roam in the city alone

She would be have been here if it wasn't for your stupid stubborn ass.. my subconscious told me

No she would have been here if she won't be so stubborn

Anyway I don't care what happens to her she can freeze to death for all I care, with that I pulled my duvet over me but sleep was far away from my eyes and I finally gave in

I took my jacket and went outside with my car keys to find that hardhead wife of mine

I started searching and as time passed I slowly started getting tensed, "god where is she?" I let out, tensed

I was passing an alley when I heard a woman shouting and screaming and it felt oddly similar to my ears, I quickly found myself following that voice and soon enough I came infront of shocking scene infront of me

There a woman was continuously was punching a man who was nearly unconscious and other two men were there groaning in pain

"You bastard what were you saying you want to have fun let me show you what fun look likes" she shouted

I quickly recognised the woman as samaira and I stepped out of my car and held back samaira by her waist

"Calm down woman" I said

She freed herself from my grasp and glared at me, "you, what are you doing here? Didn't you told that you would prefer me dieing than why would you come, huh?" She screeched

"Just shut up and sit in the car" I told her

"You know what I am sick and tired of your attitude now you are not the dictator of my life and from now on I won't follow you enough is enough, I am such a idiot to think that even now you came to search for me because you cared but now I know you are nothing but a heartless jerk and nothing else" she shouted and by now those three men have ran somewhere else

"Samaira just sit in the car and let's talk at the mansion you are creating unnecessary scene here" I said while looking here and there to see if someone was here or not

"I think you didn't got the part where I told I won't go anywhere with you, and you know what I am done staying here first thing in the morning I am going to book my flight back to India" saying this she started walking away from me

Even before she took two steps away I yanked her back using her wrist, due to force she directly landed on my chest with her arms on me

"What the hell Rudransh" she hissed

"You don't want to sit in the car willingly then it's okay don't blame me afterwards"

"What-" she stopped when I hauled her over my shoulder and started walking to my car

"What the hell Rudransh put me down" she screamed and I am sure I went deaf for a second

"Geez woman calm down it's not like I am kidnapping you" I said

When I reached my car I deposited her in the passenger seat and closed the car door

I went and sat down in the driver's seat and quickly locked my car so that he can't run away

"Rudransh open the car this instant" She screamed

"This car will be only opened when we reach our home" I say

"Your home not mine or ours" she said

We reached the mansion and as soon as I unlocked the door she jumped out of the car like she couldn't even stay in my proximity

It's not like I am dying to stay near her either

When I entered living room she was no where in sight, looks like she went in her room

I also started walking towards my room when my phone pinged, indicating I got a message

"How is the progress with her??"

######

So how was it??

Sorry for not updating yesterday was caught up in family thing

Reminding you all again I am going on a vacation from 25 to 5 so I won't be on Wattpad at all

Hope you all enjoyed today's chapter... Vote..

Signing off-

Angel

17. I Just Hate You

SAMAIRA

"Where are you going?" A sudden voice from the hallway stopped me in my tracks

"None of your concern" saying that I started walking out of this damn prison aka his mansion along with my bags

This jerk has more audacity than i thought, just as I took one step his hand seized my wrists and yanked me backward, with me resulting right on his chest

In spite I kept my hands on his chest and pushed him for him to stagger few steps back totally catching him off gaurd, "what the hell is your problem Mr Raghuvanshi" I screamed

"You, you are my problem Mrs Raghuvanshi" is there mockery I heard in his tone, my anger raised an octave

"Oh yeah right I am always your problem isn't it then why the fuck did you marry me, huh tell me, because of you my entire life got destroyed, because of you and my pathetic father who didn't even thought once before solding his daughter to a monster like you" I screamed, my dam breaking which I kept holding for past few weeks

Tears were freely flowing down my cheeks and now I can even taste the saltiness of it in my mouth and I can clearly see one emotion that I hate the most in the world, Pity.

I wiped my tears with the back of my hand and stared at him straight in the eyes, by now he have also concealed every emotion on his face and he was staring at me coldly

The living room was dead silent and only our breathing were heard in here, then his cold voice resonated in entire room,

"So sad of you to think the person you are talking about is your real father" his all time famous smirk was there

"Wh.. what do you mean?" I ask with slightly trembling voice

"That you will know soon Mrs Raghuvanshi"

#####

KRITIKA

Raghav, all my thoughts are consumed by this single man, even now when I was painting I subconsciously drew him

That same sharp brown eyes staring right at her, his delicate pinkinsh red lips which always remind her of strawberries, his chiseled jaw

Painting is one of her hobbies which she do in her leisure time, she has dedicated a whole room to her painting and no on in the house knows about

And till now this is the best painting she has made, the very own potrait of her husband

Even though she has sub consciously made it she is still happy with the results, suddenly a thought struck in my head

I should gift this potrait to raghav on our wedding anniversary

He would probably be happy, seeing how we have been past few weeks, I feeling quite excited for our upcoming first anniversary

I took the potrait and kept it safely in one of the locker in my painting room and locked it, next I went towards the basin and washed off all the paints off my hand

Then I wiped my hand on the hand towel and came outside and then locked the door, I can't afford anyone to come inside

As soon as I took three steps I bumped into a hard chest and went flying into the floor

"Oww" I whined and looked up to give a piece of mind to whoever it was but seeing who it was my words got struck in my throat

"Raghav" I whispered out

For a split second he looked down at me and then went away like nothing happened, okay what hell did happened just now

I got up from the floor and dusted myself and walked towards the direction he went off

I catched up with him and saw him entering his study room, I also entered behind and he looked a little startled and somewhat irritated

"Didn't I told you to knock before entering my study?" He asked and I slightly shivered due to fear

"What happened Raghav, you are again acting like before" I asked with a moist eyes

"Do I have some obligations to justify it to you how should I act" he retorted

"No but past few days you were so nice to me and now you are like before what happened did I do something" I couldn't help but ask with a sullen voice

"Like I said I don't want to explain it you so leave" he said

Feeling dejected, I couldn't help but ask, "Raghav don't you feel anything towards me we have been married for 7 months now but you have never treated me as your wife, why? Is something wrong?"

"Yes everything is wrong, you being in my life is wrong, my marriage with you is wrong and I just HATE YOU" and with that I could hear my heart breaking

#####

DISHA

Just as I entered the house, I could immediately sense the gloominess in the atmosphere

Kritika was sitting in the living room while staring into nothingness

I quitely sat beside her and kept my hands on her shoulder, "kritika are you okay" I couldn't help but ask in concern

Noticing her eyes anyone could say she was crying, "Nothing happened bhabhi, I am alright and you are back so early" she said

Hearing this my mind wandered back to what happened few hours back

Leaving his office, I texted harsh I am reaching our choosen destination in few minutes and then hailed a taxi and gave him the address

Sighing I leaned back and tried to relax a bit and even that was short livid, the driver informed me we have reached the park

Giving him his fare I stepped out of the taxi and started searching for a familiar face in these crowd

Aah! Found him, I started walking towards him and greeted him

"Hey" I said, smiling

"Hi, isha" he said, using the endearment he used to call me long time back

I feel little weird but didn't comment anything though

"Come, let's go"

And with that we started our fun journey in the amusement park

Time flies. And soon enough it was 5pm

As I was savouring my tub of blueberry icecream, I could feel a hard stare right at my back

Don't be ridiculous disha. This is an amusement park for godsakes so many people are roaming here

"Is it just me or somebody is actually staring at us" Harsh asked

Now it's confirmed, some creep is definitely staring

I turned back searching the creep who is staring with such a intensity and once I found out who it was my breath got hitched resulting me on chocking on my ice cream and coughing violently

"God disha be careful" he said patting my back

Once I was normal, I again looked at that exact same place and there was no one standing

Was it just my hallucination?

######

Gosh I myself even don't know what have I written

But next chapter would clear everything because it would male leads pov...

All three...

Signing off..

18. Am not your assistant

"What do you mean by he is not my real father Mr Raghuvanshi" Samaira screamed

As soon as she said that a loud ringing can be heard in the dead silent hall disturbing both of them

Realising it's his phone that has been ringing Rudransh left without even sparing samaira a glance

"Where are you going you jerk come back here" She screamed but Rudransh was long gone disappearing in the hallways of the mansion

Walking into the farthest corner of the mansion he answered the call

"I think I have messaged you yesterday?" Hearing this he sighed loudly

"Now tell me how is it going with your wife" The person on the other side asked pressing on the word 'wife' somewhat in a mocking tone

Having no other option he told the person everything that happened between him and her in past few weeks

"I don't think you will succeed if you keep up like this, tame her but don't forget you have to break her in the end, make her fall in love but never fall yourself" With this the line went dead

Fuck. I can't do this anymore, how can my brothers keep up their marriage and their facade, not even an one month passed I have started suffocating in this marriage, he thought

Here, samaira was on the verge of breaking down right in the middle of the hall

How can someone be such cold hearted man, how can he lie that the person who I have been with my whole childhood isn't my father, he is surely lying

My father may not be the best person in the world but he is still my father and my only family after my mom, I won't believe that idiotic person

Wiping the tears that have somehow escaped despite her struggle to keep them in, then she took hold of her suitcase handle once again and started walking towards the exit

I should hurry before that beast comes once again, she thought

After hailing the taxi, she instructed him to drive to the airport

After entering the airport, she checked herself in and then sat herself down at the airport

After few minutes the announcement of airplane was made and she made her way to the plane once again she found herself inside a luxurious plane but nothing compared to the Raghuvanshi's private jet that jet literally drips with money

Soon the plane took off and we were floating in the air, and that's when she closed her eyes and welcomed a dreamless slumber

----

"Where were you today" Disha asked as soon as Ryan entered his room

"Can I ask what are you doing in my room?" He asked totally ignoring her previous question

"As soon as you answer my question I will be out of your hair" she replied

"I highly doubt you have not done that for past 1 year and stuck to me like a leech so how can you leave now" he smirked

"Listen Ryan just answer where were you today afternoon and I will leave"She tried again as she really wanted to know wheather it was just her hallucination or was he really there

"I don't have free time like you to spend I run a multi million dollar company of course I would be in a meeting" he said like stating the most obvious fact

"Okay then I got my answer and good night" saying this she left

Thank God she didn't digged into it more, he thought

"Kritika where the fuck is my file" Raghav asked or yelled would be more suitable word

But kritika ignored him and didn't moved from the couch with head-phones on and her favourite playlist playing

"Are you deaf? I am asking you" This time he was standing just across her, fuming

"I am not your assistant to keep track record of all your files and I think you shouldn't depend on the wife you hate so much maybe I won't be here one day then I don't think you would be able to find anything if you don't make a habit now" she said calmly

He knew that someday it was bound to happen but hearing those words from her mouth seemed different and somewhat painful

As for kritika, she knew that after seeing the divorce papers and hearing such cold and harsh words earlier, she knew that hoping something positive to come out from this marriage is just hopeless and prepare herself for the worst

'Ring!'

A loud shrill voice of the doorbell can be heard in the entire mansion, frowning everyone thought who could so late but still kritika went to open door while everyone else came downstairs to see who it was

There were no servants as they live in servants quarter that is few meters away from the mansion

Seeing the person on the door everyone was shocked

"Samaira"

Short chapter, sorry for it!

Some more revelation would be done in next chapter

Let's see what's in store for them

Signing off-

19. I am sorry

THIRDPERSON

"Samaira you came alone? Where is Rudransh?" hearing this question from kritika made samaira burn in anger

"I don't know and I don't even care about that jerk he can rot in hell for all that I care" saying this she went upstairs in her room not wanting to hear about her good for nothing husband

Seeing the outburst of samaira everyone was shocked would be an understatement, Disha was the first one to come out of the daze and cleared her throat before speaking,

"I think she fought with him let her rest we all can talk tomorrow"

Everyone gave her a silent nod and then went to their respective rooms to get their much needed sleep

In Paris

"She left? Even after I clearly told her not too" Rudransh threw the bouquet of flowers on the floor which he bought, clearly the person on call has affected him

He had bought this to apologise to her but clearly this girl dosen't deserve it, he dugged out his phone from the pocket and dialed his assistant giving him instructions

"Book my flight to India right now"

Ending the call he went towards his room and flopped on the bed

This girl is really something different but all this dosen't matter because the same flith runs in her veins of that man

Thoughts were just running in his mind and he just can't seem to stop and what irritates him the most is all this thought are directed to one person

Samaira.

"Samaira do you wanna talk now about what happened and why you came so early" Disha asked as all three of them prepared the breakfast

"Simple, I don't want to live with that jerk anymore" she answered

"I heard from Raghav that Rudransh is also coming back like today only" Kritika said trying to decipher Samaira's reaction to it but she remained both emotionless and motionless

"Okay the breakfast is done and let's serve it" Disha said trying to divide their attention from this topic

"Okay let's go" even though there were just 5 people in total to eat, the raghuvanshi's eat like royals with full buffet to serve them

Ugh, money is really something in this world, so damn lucky they are to have so much money, these were the thoughts of all the daughter in law of the Raghuvanshi's

Right now every family member were sitting to have their first and most important meal of the day with silence surrounding them

The tension was thick that one can cut with a knife and some point it was suffocating for the three women

At last Ryan asked samaira the question she wasn't ready to answer atleast not the brother of her husband,

"Samaira did something happen between you and Rudransh"

"Yes" she answered in one word

"What?" Ryan pried

"Something I am not comfortable telling anyone" she answered, her tone held a finality

Ryan nodded and then continued, "Whatever it is I hope you both solve it your image as an daughter in law of raghuvanshi family is important, if anyone knows about that you came home alone without your husband media won't hesitate to tarnish our image so be careful" he finished

Samaira snorted in her mind and thought, yeah like I am the one that's causing problems why don't you try to control your dipshit good-for-nothing brother

Then the breakfast went like normal and both the brothers went to their respective cars which would take them to their office

After they left, everyone visibly relaxed even the maids, no one can relax in the same environment them they carry such a aura

"Disha bhabhi today I have to go somewhere today but I would come early" kritika informed

"Okay kritika" Disha replied

Tension. This word could describe the entire atmosphere in the room where three men were sitting while cold aura surrounding them

"What did you do Rudransh?" Ryan like always asked in his authoritive voice

"I just told her the truth of her father oh sorry fake father" He replied with no expression whatsoever

"Rudransh you are going extreme now don't you know how it would be and don't you forget what we agreed on our family reputation shouldn't be tarnished by this" saying this Ryan left the penthouse owned by all three of them

"Think of how to mend this Rudra" saying this Raghav also left, leaving behind fuming Rudransh

"Ugh I just hate this marriage, not even one month have passed and it's already getting suffocating for me to stay in this so called marriage" he fumed

----

In a hospital room, distinct cleanser could be smelled indicating it has been cleaned just now, a patient was laying on the white bed with small tubes attached to her body and oxygen mask attached as her only source of breathing

Another lady was sitting just beside the patient and silently talking to the patient

"It's been 8 long months Vedika and I am still living in this guilt please wake up, I can't live like this anymore with the guilt of killing someone, sending someone on their deathbed, please just wake up"

It all happened eight months ago, the dreadful incident which would be ingraved in Kritika's mind forever

Past (eight months ago)...

Today, kritika was in quite a good mood, reason, was she met her childhood friend shweta after a very long time and had lot of fun with her and had a good time

Humming a tune of her favourite song she happily drived her personal favourite car gifted to her by her dearest uncle

It was a red colour Ferrari and yeah for your information she loves car

A sudden ringing of her phone broke her thinking trance and she quickly fetched her phone from the backseat and pressed on answer button

"Hello, Rishabh how are you" Rishabh was her favourite and only cousin, he was her uncle's son

"I am fine what about you" he asked

As she was driving while talking a girl suddenly appeared before her car and before she could hit brakes it was too late and due to the impact the other girl's body went flying into some distance

Present....

And that's why Kritika bought her here and seeing her wallet she came to know her name and every other details

Sensing it was time to leave she got up and took her handbag which she bought with herself and left her ward

Walking down the lonely hallway as she kept her in the vip ward as she only wanted high class service for her

"Excuse me ma'am" A sudden voice halted my steps

Turning around she came face to face with a young doctor probably in his late 20's

She quickly recognised him he is was one of the doctors who are treating Vedika

"Is there something?" I asked

"Actually, the life support that we are using on Vedika I think is of no use and it can come in use for someone else I don't think we should wait anytime more" he replied

"I think the hospital is getting their bills paid so till the time I am paying do your job" saying this she left

----

Sitting in the dining hall to have their last meal of the day everyone was once again greeted with silence

Due to this Samaira couldn't help but remember what happened in the afternoon when that jerk happened appear back

"Ohh you came back so sad I actually thought you won't come" samaira said in somewhat fake sad tone

"Looks like you are very sad I came back isn't it" he asked

"Of course I actually thought I could live peacefully for few days" she retorted

"Now that you have came back what are you planning to do wet my bed again or push me into the tub or-"

"I am sorry" Samaira abruptly stopped hearing the words the the man infront of her just spewed

"Wait, what did you just said?" She asked just to confirm her ears aren't playing tricks on her

"I am sure you heard it in the first time but then though I said I am sorry" he said

"Are you sure you are saying it to me or are there some invisible spirit that I can't see" Samaira asked while looking here and there for the spirit she just mentioned

"But if you are saying this to me then I just have one thing to say-" she then started walking and stopped just across him with their chest touching and her lips brushing along the lobe of his ears

"- shove that sorry upto your ass" saying this she left for washroom like always leaving the youngest son of Raghuvanshi's in daze

God, Samaira can't you control your mouth why do you speak so much now this jerk will definitely kill you... Samaira thought while evading the deathly glare of her husband sitting right across her

Let's just pray he doesn't murder me tonight.. Samaira thought and started munching her dinner along with others

----

This chapter was in my draft from last week yet I couldn't complete

Hope you enjoyed today's chapter

Many of you are asking when everything would be revealed but guys have patience everything would be done at its own pace

Signing off-

20. An accidental kiss

THIRDPERSON

Samaira was so nervous that instead of eating the dinner she was fidgeting with spoon in her hand and nervously bouncing her legs against the table

A shriek left her mouth as she felt a hand against her knees and it startled everyone sitting there

"Samaira are you okay?" Disha asked and she nodded

Then she felt that the hands belongs to none other than her husband who was sitting right across her and staring at her, like indicating to stop her from what she was doing

Getting the warning she stopped it and resumed her eating

How can this dumbass keep his hands on my knees and how the hell did his hands reached across looks like his hand is lot more longer than I thought,

Samaira was so distracted with her thoughts that she didn't even noticed that everyone is done with their dinner until kritika shook her and broke her reverie

"Wanna sit here whole night, Samaira?" Kritika joked

"Ahh... What?"

"Are you alright?" Disha asked seriously concerned as she was nervous whole dinner

"No no I am fine" she said and started eating her dinner in a fast pace, she completed her dinner in just 5 minutes, shocked kritika and disha could only stare at her

"If you were so hungry you could have told us" listening this Samaira just laughed and the other two joined her

"Okay you both go and sleep I will tell sneha to do the dishes I am too tired to do anything" Disha said and went away to tell the maid for doing the dishes while the other two went to their respective rooms

Fear and nervousness which went away for few moments while talking to both the ladies came rushing back and enveloped Samaira and got embedded in her bones

She may show that she was strong and firm but still compared to his strength she is no more bigger than a ant and now when the previous strength is gone she is shivering as leaf

Taking a deep breath she pushed open the bedroom door and was prepared for the lashing of her husband but instead of harsh words what she heard was calm breathing and light snoring

Samaira bit her lips to contain her laughter due to the scene infront, her husband who is always tough like a stone is now snoring with his lips slightly parted and his blanket thrown somewhere on the floor

Not even realising it Samaira took her phone and clicked his picture and when she realised what she did she asked herself ; why the hell did I took his picture

When she was about to delete the picture a thought came in her mind, I can use this picture to blackmail him sometime in the future

Thinking about that she didn't delete but even saved it in her drive incase it gets deleted

After that she did her night routine and quickly slept on the second bed just beside his bed

Being tired due household chores sleep quickly engulfed her in its embrace

----

As Disha entered her bedroom she noticed something was not right but what

She went in her closet and quickly checked her clothes and like expected nothing was there

"Ahh ryaaannn I will not spare you today you jerk" I hastily walk towards his room, today he has signed his death certificate who told him to move my belongings

She knew for sure it was his doing, when did he got that done I was in the house for whole day, she thought

She barged in his room without knocking and she regretted it because there he came out of the bathroom with water droplets still intact on his body and hair dripping with water making his body more wet and dropping inside his towel which was hanging on his waist

"Ahh" she screamed and quickly turned back covering her eyes

"What the hell Ryan" she screamed

"Well I should ask you that" he replied

"How would I know you will come half naked atleast you could wear a robe" she screamed thank god all rooms in this mansion are soundproof

"You would know if you would have knocked like any other sane person and about the robe it's my house and my room I can wear whatever I want and now you can turn around I am dressed" She turned around cautiously and peeked through her fingers to see wheather he is lying or not

Once satisfied he is fully dressed she removed her hands and glared at him full intensity

"Woah did I do something to receive such a glare" even though he was asking disha knew he already knows the reason for her arrival

"Why did you moved my belongings back here Mr Raghuvanshi" she asked making sure to keep her voice stern and firm

"I think you already know the reason Mrs Raghuvanshi" hearing the word mrs raghuvanshi from his mouth felt like he was mocking her in some way but still trying to stay unaffected by this she asked

"I think I quite don't know the reason so please enlighten me"

"Tch and here I thought I bought myself a smart wife" was he insulting me directly or complementing me indirectly, Disha thought and decided to go with the former

"Listen Ryan please do not test me so spill the reason don't fu- play around" disha said correcting herself

"Why did you stop cursing yourself infront of me you can continue" he replied with a calm facial expression

"Oh really then thank you so much for granting me such a precious opportunity I hope you don't regret it Mr Ryan Raghuvanshi" she said back which turned Ryan a little confused but still his facade of calm and composed didn't broke

And just like that the dam in Disha broke "You are shittiest person on this earth whom I was cursed to marry in the worst time of my life I thought you were my knight in shining armour in those times but who knew you were wolf if sheeps clothing, you despicable jerk" along with her words her tears broke too and she left the room in anger and locked herself in the previous room she was staying in

Seeing such outburst shocked Ryan but it was somewhat expected because every human at certain points have their breaking point and this was hers, let it be, he thought and pretending like nothing happened he called it a night

----

Peaceful that's how she felt after taking the much needed bath after the whole day in staying that sticky and sweaty clothes

"Kritika when will you come out it's been half an hour"

Was that worry in his voice?, Hah keep on dreaming kritika, he might be waiting so that he can take his turn

"Jeez, coming you can't even let me bath in peace"

Wrapping the towel around my body and one around my hair, yep probably not the best decision as it was quite chilly in the night but she didn't had any option due to all the sweat in her hair

As she was taking quite hurried steps and opened the door with a hurry not expecting the hunk of man right infront of her and collided with him and due to his imbalance both fell onto the floor but that's not what caught kritika's attention it was the fact that their lips were on top of each other

AND THEY WERE KISSING!

Hehe! Sorry for ending the chapter their

Hope you enjoyed today's chapter

Comment your thoughts..

Signing off for now-

21. Rudransh, You pervert

THIRDPERSON

Startled, kritika quickly started getting up but due to slippery floor she slipped again and their lips came in contact again

This time she again got up but with caution and quickly explained herself, "I didn't mean it to happen it was purely accidental" her back was to him for the whole time

Instead of hearing a harsh reply she only heard door closing and then shower running in the bathroom

Realising that he went inside, she let out a sigh of relief and went to get ready for the night in her sleepwear

Laying down on the bed she couldn't help but think what happened just now, the kissing scene playing right infront of her eyes and only one thing in her mind

I Lost My First Kiss To Raghav Raghuvanshi....

Soft rays were the first thing which greets Disha every morning and the sole reason why her sleep get disturbed

The first thought which hit her hard was the fact the she cursed RYAN RAGHUVANSHI

She have certainly signed her death certificate by doing this but she doesn't feel even an ounce of regret of doing that after all he was the one who gave her the permission to curse

But he gave the permission to curse infront of him not curse him

Yeah, yeah whatever what is done is done no going back now

"Okay disha be brave and embrace what you did atleast you feel good after what you did" preparing herself she stood up and started doing her morning routine until it clicked her

She hadn't bought any clothes due to her heat of the moment from yesterday

'ugh now I have to face him, can my life get any more better' do not miss the sarcasm please

Unwillingly Disha found herself infront of the room's door that she wish she never sees

Taking a deep breath to steady herself she pushed open the door but at the same time the door opened from inside and what's next she is about to fall ahhh-

But wait I have not fallen yet, she thought

When she opened her eyes there he was standing and his arms snaked around her waist

HIS ARMS AROUND HER WAIST.. disha quickly regained her composure and stood upright

"Thank you" acknowledging his help she thanked him and went to take her clothes and she was soon leaving but not before-

"I expect my clothes back in the room I staying just like you bought them here without my permission" purposely stressing on the world without my permission

[Time skip to breakfast]

"Holi is upcoming next week I hope everyone knows what to do" Ryan voice resonated in the obviously silent dining room

Everyone nodded except Samaira as she was unknown what to do and how to do it

"If you don't mind Ryan Bhai then can you please tell me what I have to do on Holi" Samaira asked, confused

"Just help disha and kritika" he answered

"So disha bhabhi what we usually do"

"We three have to see the decoration,food and etc means we have to keep everything in order on that day"

"Oh okay" she answered back

And just like that their day went like always, uneventful

Night soon fell upon and everyone once again gathered to have their last meal of the day

Is there some sort of rule to not talk here why is everyone always dead silent ,Samaira couldn't help but wonder

Like always variety of food have been presented on the dining table resembling a free buffet

"How many people are we inviting Ryan for the Holi party" Disha broke the silence with her question

"I will send out the invitation this time you handle the rest no need to do anything about the invitation" and once again the table fell dead silent

----

As soon as kritika entered her room she cursed her luck in her mind

There he was standing just coming out of the bathroom with just a towel, A TOWEL

Don't we have enough robes in the bathroom for this man can't he cover his full body with the robe and come out dressed decently

Whatever, even though he is sculpted by the god himself, I won't look at him

Going through her closet kritika kept on her work despite him just standing there with barely nothing

"Woah Kritika go out I am standing here just in towel"

"Tch, Raghav listen I don't care weather you are standing in a towel or downright naked, I am just trying to find my nightwear and then I will straightaway go to take a shower so need to be so shy like a newlywedded wife, understood" saying this she found my nightwear and went in the washroom like she mentioned

'this woman, ugh' Raghav thought

Disgusting, that's what Samaira thought as soon as she entered the room

The room was smelling full of cigarettes and alcohol and she hated this smell because it always reminded her of a past, a very disgusting past

Following the scent she came into the very own balcony attached to the room with Mr. Jerk sitting there or more like drowning himself in alcohol and cigarettes

"I didn't knew Mr Raghuvanshi you were so eager to make me a widow" She taunted

"I didn't knew you cared Mrs Raghuvanshi" he replied with his back still facing her

"Care? Ofcourse Mr Raghuvanshi afterall it's a fact that both cigarette and alcohol reduces your life span and I don't want you die early and that's what a wife should do isn't it, care for her husband" there wasn't a bit of care in her tone, but you could find mockery in her tone

But after that everything happened in a blink of an eye and she found herself pinned on the nearest wall

"What the heck are you trying to do" samaira screamed

"What a wife should do huh? Why don't you start doing other wifely duties huh?" His hands roaming on her body igniting a fire but Samaira stood strong

Her face was flushed and she thanked heavens because no lights were in the balcony and he couldn't see her flushed face

His hands weren't stopping and Samaira brain has suddenly stopped working and she suddenly blurted out-

"I have my period"

He suddenly stopped and she let out a sigh of relief

"Period? I have heard a fact somewhere that a orgasm helps with period cramps, wanna try?" He smirked and Samaira froze

When the words got registered in her mind she screamed-

"Rudransh, You pervert"

Got to know to many facts today *smiles*

Hope you enjoyed today's chapter

Sorry for not updating earlier

Next update: after we reach 30k or 50 comments on this chapter

Signing off

22. Forever In My Memories

[THIRDPERSON]

"Bhabhi"

"Hmm"

"Can a orgasm really help with period cramps?" Samaira asked and the tea that kritika was sipping immediately flew out

Taking a tissue she cleaned herself and then stared at Samaira like asking without words ' what the hell are you asking '

"Samaira from where did you get this piece of information? Huh" Disha who was standing there equally shocked, inquired

From my perverted husband, she wanted to shout but decided against it as it would be too embarassing

"I read it somewhere that's why I asked if you both will know by any chance?" Unsurity was dripping from her tone

"Listen Samaira having sex is one thing but having sex on period is an entirely different thing, some people may gross out thinking of that and in this women are involved too so I don't think anyone has tried it out physically certainly not us so we can't tell you" Kritika tried to explain as calmly as possible while disha never expected that they three would be talking about sex in such few days of knowing each other

"Mam, sirs are sitting and waiting for the food" a servant broke their conversation

Nodding Disha signaled the other two to bring the other breakfast and brought out some breakfast herself

Everyone settled down and the servants started serving the breakfast and everyone patiently waited for the servants to finish the servings on everyone's plate and then soon everyone digged in

The breakfast went like any other day, dead silent and by now Samaira was also accomodated to it

And just like that everyone started doing their daily work

Everything was going on its usual pace but a phone call disturbed everything

"What? Which hospital, tell me I am coming immediately" Disha frantically asked the other person

Once she got her answers and ended the phone call, she immediately got surrounded by the other two ladies

"What happened Bhabhi?" Kritika asked

"Rud_ Rudransh he got a allergic reaction and he is in a serious condition in the ICU"

Hearing this everyone immediately left for the hospital Ryan mentioned

After reaching there, Kritika abruptly stopped noticing this is the same hospital she has admitted Vedika

"Kritika what are you waiting for??"

Noticing her standing there, Disha pulled her with herself

Reaching the reception disha asked,

"Where is Rudransh Raghuvanshi admitted?"

But the receptionist was on the phone and ignored them, not just once but thrice

Losing her patience Samaira banged her hand on the desk and practically yelled

"Rudransh Raghuvanshi room no, right now"

And this got her attention and gave them the room no, stuttering with fear

"Room no 2, Vip floor take that lift"

With that those three soon stood infront of the room along with the others

"What happened to him?" Disha askedwhile taking deep breaths as all of them came running

"Doctors said he had a severe allergic reaction, who made today's food?" Ryan asked

"I made it" Samaira came forward

"Did you by chance added peanut in his food"

"Yeah, as I don't like those chunks of peanuts I crushed.." Samaira realised what she had done if she had added whole pieces of it someone would have noticed and stopped Rudransh from eating but she crushed it and no one noticed

After knowing her mistake she stood still to get scolding from Rudransh's elder brothers

Few minutes passed but nobody said anything to her so she looked at them with questioning face and couldn't help but ask, "aren't you going to scold me? Because of me your brother is here"

"Why should we scold you, when our servents who have lived with us for almost whole lives can make such mistake then you have only lived with us for a month" Raghav replied

At the same time a doctor came out Rudransh ward and said

"He is now in a stable condition but due to the allergy some rash would still be there on his body, he should take some hot water bath, and as this is the second time of his allergy reaction and so severe he will still feel weak for sometime so he needs to rest, that's all" and with that he left and everyone entered his ward

There he lying with small, thin pipes attached to his body, he naturally looked very weak

His two brothers went to his both sides and fired questions on him

"How are you?"

"Do you feel fine?"

"You want anything?"

Everything is on one side and the bond this brothers share is one side

After Rudransh assured that he doesn't need anything, then only their train of questions stopped

"We would have stayed for more time but Rudransh we need to leave, for some time being Samaira will stay with you" and that's what sealed Samaira's fate to stay with Rudransh for almost for entire day

And she too accepted it as somewhere in her heart she knew this was because of her and he is lying in the hospital because of her

Silently she went near the table with fruits provided from the hospital, yeah special treatment for special patient

Sitting on the couch she picked up a apple and started slicing it with the knife too provided by hospital, once done she got up and sat down near him and spoke little softly

"Rudransh here I sliced the apple, can you get up or should I help you?"

Without replying her, he got up by himself even wincing in the process but still not taking her help

Taking the plate from her hand he started chewing without taking in the account of the person he sliced it for him

How rude! Samaira exclaimed in her mind but still controlled her growing anger and tried to apologise

"Rudransh I am sorry I didn't knew you had allergy to peanut I will keep it mind next time"

And do you know what he did next, he fucking snorted and then full on laughed at her apology

"What the fuck are you laughing for?" Samaira shouted unable to control her anger, if anyone would see her now they would definitely think she resembles an angry bull, with face full red one could even see steams coming out her ear

"Can you say that again I want to record it I will forever keep it as my memory" he replied

She grinded her teeth, this scoundrel she was apologising and she is thinking about this stupid thing

"Go to hell and rot there Rudransh Raghuvanshi, stupid jerk" huffing out air in irritation she went and sat on the couch

They both like that for quite some time and rather than silence being awkward it was comfortable and peaceful

And just like that Samaira dozed off and now Rudransh observed her while resting his upper body against the headboard

She looks quite good, even beautiful but only if she can keep her mouth shut like this always it would be much better, Rudransh thought

Only if Samaira would have heard his thought she would have replied, Shutting your mouth goes both way idiot you too need to shut it

----

So much work, Ryan thought

Sudden opening of the door caught his attention and once he looked up, his lips curved up into one of the rarest smile

"Shlok bro you here, come sit" he said happily

Shlok, cousin of the three brothers he is the eldest among the six sons of Devdutt Raghuvanshi, yonger brother Ryan, Raghav and Rudransh father, they have another uncle who is eldest among Devdutt and their father, Rishabh is his name, Shlok and his brothers are a little close with these three...

(A/n : (spoiler) Next would be Devdutt sons story 6 couples ahh I am excited)

"Ryan my brother, you are the same as before looks like your wife isn't feeding you" Shlok joked

"She isn't my caretaker, I can feed myself and besides you yourself haven't changed much" and like always he didn't understood my joke, Shlok sighed

"Anyways what brings you here" Ryan questioned

"Aarush and Arpita's birthday next week come with everyone, yeah only that now I have to get going see you next week"

And with that he left just like he came leaving Ryan with his own set of thoughts

He couldn't help but remember what happened last time when Disha went with him to the twins birthday party, Nothing but insults followed her as she wasn't particularly someone famous and those shitty people thought she doesn't deserve to be raghuvanshi's daughter-in-law

After it got too much Ryan gave them his signature glare but that time it hundred times much icier and it sent the signal to the gossiping ladies to immediately shut up, but anyone could still have seen the gloomy look Disha had the entire party

Sighing he thought he would think at night wheather he wants to tell Disha or not

For now let's focus on the work that's pending, he thought and then again got immensed in the work

----

Night time were boring for Kritika especially when her phone's battery had died down and her husband is just another reincarnation of statue who is just staring at the ceiling without exchanging any word with her

Thinking she should be the to take the initiative, she asked, "Raghav how is work going nowadays you don't tell me anything"

"Good"

"How was the dinner today did you like it?"

"Yes"

"Will you go to work tomorrow?"

"Yes"

Seeing him lost in his wonderland, she thought a way of bringing him out of it and giggled to herself

"Are you an idiot?"

"Yes"

"Are you a jerk?"

"Yes"

After that he blinked few times then looked at kritika who looked at him innocently like she didn't said that just now

"What did said just now?"

"I suppose you are not deaf" saying this she quickly escaped the room as anger was radiating from him

Laughing she thought she would forever in my memory but suddenly tears escaped and started rolling down her cheeks, thank god no one is to see me in this state she thought

Along with such thing she would keep many more memories like her seeing the divorce papers, him saying that he hates her and many more

Laughing bitterly she sat on of the dining table chairs and kept her head against the table,

Looks like I am really pathetic when it comes to him, she thought and laughed bitterly.

____

So guys we reached the 30k reads target and I updated..

Just like I gave the spoiler above next book will be about Devdutt sons

There would be six couples, I am so excited to write *giggling*

So anyways let's come on this story, do comment and let me know about the chapter

Target for next chapter : 300 votes

Signing off-

23. Woman who saved Arpita

THIRDPERSON

"Ugh, Samaira how many clothes are you going try atleast take a rest or let us take a rest because we don't know about you but we are fucking tired" Kritika groaned

Right now they three are shopping in one of the most famous mall because just this morning they were informed that they all need to attend Shlok's kids birthday party, at first they were confused as just Disha knows who is Shlok and she explained it to them and right after that they were given a black card by Ryan and told to shop whatever they like, like for the first time after they got married here, all three of them thought

So of course samaira grabbed the opportunity and now dragging the other two with her with one shop to another

"I am done for all of us" yeah the biggest mistake they made to give her chance to buy their clothes and accessories too and half of their ended here just because of that

"Finally let's go back I am dying here" Disha interjected

"Oh my god you both get tired so soon you should exercise a bit" Samaira laughed but shut up as soon as she noticed both women glaring at her

Taking all their things, paying the necessary money or more like forcing them to accept,

It surely has perks to be a millionaire wife, isn't it, Samaira thought

"Okay let's get going"

"Can't we get to eat something eat first" now who can argue samaira so to not delay anymore they went to the food court and ordered their food

They ordered some veg lasagne and Roasted Ratatouille Pasta along with some potato wedges and coke

After having a heartful meal, they left the mall and went straight for the home

.....

[After some time, 5 hours before the party]

Samaira was getting ready while smiling more like smirking like waiting for something to happen

"SAMAIRA" both the women came barging into her room and they half angry half confused

"Samaira what have bought for us" Disha asked

"A gown for the party what happened don't you like it" Samaira replied

"Like it? It's so revealing we are going in children party, for godsakes" Kritika said

"Oh come on, I am sure those women in party would be particularly naked to attract rich people no one would care if we wear this type of clothes, we would practically considered conservative infront of those women, we should try these type of clothes once in a while" Samaira saying closed her door and pushed them to change into the clothes she chose

After they both changed, Samaira whistled and couldn't help but say

"I knew it, I chose the perfect dress, oh god I am proud of myself" she said while patting her own back

"Oh god Samaira please don't whistle like a hooligan, it creeps me out" kritika exclaimed and finally after 5 minutes she calmed down and changed into her own clothes

"Okay now as we are ready, I will call the hairstylist and makeup artist upstairs here" Making a call on her phone she called them upstairs and after few minutes they too came upstairs

It was Sana, the hairstylist and Tina, the makeup artist and yeah they both are sisters

After opening the door, they both were dumbfounded like literally they had their lips parted and one could even see drool dripping from the corner of their mouth

Unconsciously both Disha and Kritika shrunk back due to their gaze while Samaira stood unaffected

"Girls you better start working and make us hot, well we are already hot but make us more hot like smoking hot" Samaira said and the girls happily started working and giving the compliments now and then

"Mam your hair is so smooth"

"Mam you have such smooth skin tone"

"Your lips are so full and pink and kissable"

Okay, now that creeped me out, Kritika thought as the last one was said to her

Sensing what she had said had made the environment awkward, Tina laughed awkwardly and both of them continued doing their work without saying anything

After full 3 hours they were done and after they left but not before Disha paying them

"Dang, they really made us smoking hot" Samaira said observing herself in the mirror as well as the other two

Disha's look^^^

Kritika's look^^^

Samaira's look^^^

"It's 6 right now and the party starts at 8 right so we have much time" Kritika said

"Nope we don't have much time, it's takes 1 hour to reach where the party is held, so the men would be coming at 7 and we will right away" Samaira replied

"But how do you know where the party is held?" Disha questioned

"Simple, I asked my good-for-nothing husband" she replied nonchalantly

One hour passed just like that and right now they all were leaving for the venue

The men didn't did anything other than changing their three piece suit and setting their watch along with adding few other accessories

As today's birthday party theme was red, all three of them went with a combination with red and black

Even though seeing their wives they were stunned still they didn't say anything, well except Rudransh

"You look better today" He poked at Samaira

"Sorry to say this but you look even uglier today" she jabbed back

"Ouch! You hurted me Mrs Raghuvanshi"

"I fully intended to do that Mr Raghuvanshi" she threw a sweet smile at him and they walked towards their car along with others

This time they decided to take one car as it would be more convenient, as they are going to a family party and arriving together would be more proper

Gifts and every other things were bought by the men only, and already placed the back of the car

....

Once reached the place where the party was held, everyone got down one by one, and went inside with their respective pair

Even at the children birthday party, there were swarm of reporters and they started clicking crazily once a family entred the venue

Same happened once Ryan, Raghav and Rudransh entered with their wives

Entering inside, the three women let out a breath of relief cause no reporter were allowed inside

As soon as they entered a girl came running and clinged to Disha's leg

She had black hair and big doe eyes with brown eyes, sparkling after seeing disha and with her clothes she seems to be the birthday girl

(Oozing elegance (□□□))

"Disha chachi, why did you came so late, you know even mom was waiting for you"

"I am sorry I kept you waiting, my dear Arpita" Disha said smiling

"Arpita do not run, how many time should I remind you' A boy said and stood infront of Arpita with a little bit stern look but still looking at dotingly like a brother

"I am sorry Bhai but see who came" Arpita was eager to tell her brother

Looks like these cousins are really close with each other, Kritika thought

Looking at them, Aarush suddenly got shocked seeing a woman,

"You aren't you that same woman who saved Arpi that day" he said pointing towards Samaira

......How's the chapter??

Who's clothes is best?? Spent too much time searching for them, especially the women's..

Sorry I told in my announcement that two update would come but I am updating this today and next chapter on Wednesday

.

24. Princess Dosen't Cry

THIRDPERSON

"I don't remember doing anything like that" Samaira replied

"2 years back, when we were getting off from our family car to go to our school, Arpita crossed the road in the green light and you saved her from getting hit by the car" Aarush explained

And Samaira could recall small snippets of what he explained and then smiled when she fully recalled a girl full two pigtails frightened and freezed in the middle of the road and car honking, and the girl do looks like the Arpita standing infront of her

"Oh now I remember, but it's shocking you still remember it you also would be quite small isn't it" Samaira asked Aarush

"My brother is very smart, he remembers everything, sometimes I wonder if he is even my brother, I hardly remember anything, just like now, I came here to bring you all to Maa and other Chachi's, let's go" seeing the cute little girl babbling, everyone burst out laughing

...

"Disha, you all came, come here" A woman nearly in her early 30's called out for Disha and the other two women walking behind Arpita

"Maa, see Rudransh Chachu and Raghav Chachu also got married and here are my two new Chachi"

"Kritika and Samaira right, sorry we couldn't come in your weddings" Another women called out to them

"Yep, and you?" Samaira asked

"My name is Aadhya, Hriday's wife, and this is Meera Shlok Bhai's wife, Aaru and Arpu's mom, and then this is our cutie Vedika, Agasthya's wife" She introduced herself

So weird even though we are from the same family, my good for nothing husband never told me about them and now we are getting introduced like some strangers now I am feeling fucking weird here, Samaira thought

"Mom when will we cut the cake?" Arpita chimed in

"It will happen in some time, my dear papita" Vedika said smiling

"Chachi don't call me that" she made yucky face

"Okay my dear pumpkin"

...

"Bhabhi I am feeling all stuffy here, I will take a walk and come" informing Kritika who was sitting in the nearest chair to her, Samaira left

Walking for a few distance, she came into one of the lavishly decorated balcony

Just as she was about to take a step, she discovered someone crying in the distance

Rounding around the corner, she came across a crying Arpita, who was sobbing very badly but still not loud enough for anyone to here

"Arpita beta, what happened why are you crying and that too sitting here?"

Hiccuping, she looked up and faced Samaira with silent tears escaping her eyes

"Those men, they ins_ulted maa and dad, sayi_ng my maa is just a substitute who wi_ll run away leaving my dad ju_st like my birth mother" she answered, still hiccuping and crying in between

"Arpita come on standup_" Samaira took ahold of her hand and helped her standing up

"_And wipe your tears, and always remember, a princess dosen't cry and you are and always will be a princess"

"And let's go back to the banquet and have some fun" Samaira said, smirking

...

"Who is that man who talked like that about your parents, Arpita?"

She pointed her fingers, and a man in his early 40s came in her view

'Ahh, Mr Bakshi' Samaira thought, the reason she knew him because her father took her once to a party and that's where she met him

Utterly disgusting man!

A waiter was just passing by, stopping and taking a glass of water from him, Samaira sent that waiter away

Walking towards Mr Bakshi, she tapped on his shoulder, and once he turned around-

Splash!

Samaira dumped all the water over him and tossed the glass away

"This was to wake you up, Mr Bakshi, coming in the party hosted by Raghuvanshi's family and yet berating their eldest son and daughter-in-law, looks like people like you have no shame nowadays isn't it" She started shouting

"You bitch" He lifted his hands to hit her, but Samaira was fast enough to hold his hands and twist it behind his back and kick on his back and brought him on his knees with her heels digging in his calf

"You old hag, trying to compete Samaira in small puny games like this, don't ever forget, I am self defence expert, and can break all bone in your body in mere 5 minutes, do not mess with me"

"Samaira!" Ah, dear husband has arrived, Samaira thought and turned around with a smirk

Not just Rudransh, but everyone was standing there and seeing Meera, Arpita quickly ran to her

"Maa"

"What is happening here?" Shlok asked

Hearing this Arpita narrated everything, and after that they took Mr Bakshi or rather dragged out would be right word on how he was taken out

Samaira walked towards Arpita and crouched down to her level, and smiled,

"Listen Arpita, when anyone disrespect you or anyone who is dearest to you, never cry, stand straight, look straight into their eyes and give them a hard punch and never back down, because like I said a princess dosen't cry, she always fights back" when today Arpita was crying, Samaira saw her childhood in her

Back in the past she was also like this, crying somewhere in the corner and no one cared about her, now she didn't wanted anyone to be like that

"Okay, everyone, cake cutting time" 'I think this is shaurya, youngest son of Devdutt Raghuvanshi' Samaira thought

"Let's go Arpita and Aarush, the thing you were waiting for desperately, your cake" with that Meera Bhabhi took them away and slowly everyone left, except Disha and Kritika Bhabhi

"Samaira did something happened in your past, when you were talking to Arpita you were quite sad?" Disha asked

"Yeah you can talk to us" Kritika said and Samaira couldn't help but smile

"It's so weird, isn't it? The one whom I married dosen't care about me, heck my own parents didn't care about me so what can I accept from him, but here you both are asking me the things which no one saw but you two did, sometimes I wonder in such short span of time we all three grew such a strong bond

But how and when?" Samaira couldn't help but wonder

"Maybe because willingly or unwillingly we all three are in the same situation, maybe because no one can understand our pain, maybe because people outside think we live lavishly but reality behind the closed doors is quite different from it, that's why" Disha said with a pained smile on her face

Samaira couldn't help but take her in a hug and Kritika joined both of them, all of them dealing with their own inner battles but still keeping a smile on their faces

"No matter what happens, let's promise that we will always have each other's back" kritika said and forwarded her hand and they both nodded and kept their hands on hers, like sealing a promise

And that was the day their real and pure friendship started

...

Oh, how much I loved this chapter, but did you all liked it too??

If yes, the please do vote and comment

Signing off-

25. Bhabhi, it's investment

THIRDPERSON

"This, no this, no no actually show me this" right now Samaira is sitting in a jwellery shop along with the other two and choosing a ring for all three of them

"Great choice mam, this ring is made with finest quality of dimond and it's all precisely cut to make a wonderful design"

"What can I say, I naturally have a good choice" Samaira flaunted infront of the sales person

"Can I ask you Samaira why have we came for the shopping again when we just went for the shopping 3 days ago" Kritika said, yeah the birthday party was done three days ago and many things happened that day, like the three women friendship got more stronger and harmonious and when there was couple dance on the stage, Samaira might have stepped on to her husband foot accidentally

"Oh come on bhabhi, they gave us their credit card, the least we can do is spent as much money we can until they take the cards back, and trust me this types of investment are useful, we can sell this if we ever run from the Raghuvanshi's mansion" Samaira smiled, and her gaze was dreamy like she was literally dreaming the scenario of running away

Snap!

Disha snapping her finger infront of her broke her dream

"And by buying investment you mean a diamond ring worth ₹ 5,00,000"

"Of course just think once we would sell this it would be wonderful" she replied and then ordered the sales person to pack all the three rings she decided

Suddenly Samaira's phone rang and it was her dearest hubby. Note the sarcasm please

"Samaira, what the heck you have spent ₹5,00,000 in one day, what the hell did you buy?"

"Jeez dear hubby, don't shout so much do you want your wifey to go deaf or what, and as for the money, why are you shouting so much I had just spent some money which won't even bring a dent in the Raghuvanshi's net worth or your company is going in a loss, Mr Raghuvanshi, if it's then please do tell me,

Or else you know reporters too well isn't it, tomorrow there would be their headlines would be #The high and mighty Raghuvanshi heirs can't even give their wifes 5,00,000 to spend# and I know you don't want that to happen, okay bye, my energy got drained talking to you I will buy something to eat" without giving him a chance to speak she hanged up

"Okay now I am really hungry let's go and eat" saying this she started walking, but seeing they were not walking she stopped and turned around

"Don't worry too much, like I said it's an investment, and like I mentioned earlier it won't even put a dent in their net worth and besides we ladies atleast deserve this much, and for another thing we didn't had any marriage ring what would people say if they saw this,

That Raghuvanshi's are so poor can't even provide their daughter-in-laws a single wedding ring" She finished with a smile

"Actually you are right, if not as an accesories then we can keep this jwellery as a investment" Disha agreed

"Of course who knows what happens tomorrow, perks of having rich husbands we know what to invest where" Kritika added and thus all three of them left the mall happily, but not before grabbing something to eat

...

"Oh, today you came here very early" Kritika exclaimed, seeing Raghav sitting on the bed with his laptop on his lap

"Did you go shopping today?" He asked, lifting his head

"Yes along with Disha Bhabhi and Samaira" she replied

"What did you buy then?" He asked

"Oh we all bought a ring for each of us" she replied

"So where is it?"

"It's will come tomorrow, there was some modifications to do for the ring size" she again replied, and then walked towards wardrobe and took out her clothes to wear at home

"Did you bought anything else?" He asked, did I hear anticipation in his voice, Kritika thought but immediately dismissed that thought, huh the Raghav Raghuvanshi, the GREAT RAGHAV RAGHUVANSHI won't have anticipation for anything, have you seen his face always so cold and aloof, these were kritika's thought

"No why did you wanted something?" She asked

"Why would I want something, I just wanted to know how much all you spent" he immediately said or more like defended himself and Kritika detected some anger in it

Ahh, expenses of course what else did I expect

With that kritika went inside the washroom to change her clothes and with that Raghav's face crumpled

...

"Here" Samaira handed her husband a wristwatch she bought with her own money so he can't taunt her like

'Bought me gift with my own money huh' Samaira could totally see it happening

"What is this?"

"Are you blind or an idiot, either you can't see what is this or you can't understand what it is after seeing it isn't it"

"Woah no need to get so hyped up, what I meant why you bought it for me?" He asked

"Cause , I thought a idiot will surely look a little less idiotic once he wears it" she answered

"You are calling me a idiot?" He asked dumbfounded

"No I am calling myself a idiot" she added sarcastically

"You, just wait" with that started the tickling match between the two

"Hah, st_o_p Rud_ran_sh" Samaira panted

"Oh looks like I found your spot, huh" and he kept tickling her

"St_op"

"First say I am not an idiot"

"Okay_ you are_ not an id_iot" and then he stopped

They were still in that position, Samaira below Rudransh both staring in each other eyes, like staring into each other souls, Samaira could feel her breath getting erratic due to them being close and Rudransh was no different

And just as she was about to push him_

"Samaira come down- oh I am so sorry" Disha entered and mistook their position for something else

"I kept knocking but no one answered so I thought Samaira was in washroom, I am so sorry" saying this she left

"Get aside" Samaira pushed Rudransh aside and then went downstairs to meet Disha

...

I was thinking of adding their kissing scene, but couldn't bring myself to it, atleast for now

Anyways, how was it??

Don't forget to vote and comment

Signing off-

26. Holi is here

THIRDPERSON

Lag Ja Gale Ki Phir Ye Hasin Raat Ho Na Ho

Shaayad Phir Is Janam Men Mulaaqaat Ho Na Ho

Lag Jaa Gale ...

Humming the tune and singing along the lyrics of her one of the fav song, Disha was lost in her own world

Sitting in the balcony of the bedroom, eyes closed while letting herself lose, without a care of outside world

She was so lost in the music that she didn't even noticed Ryan sitting onto the chair next to her

"Looks like you are really enjoying the music"

Hearing his voice, Disha was a little startled and subconsciously stood upright and thought,

I was really enjoying the music, but then you came

"Yes, one of my favourite songs" she replied

"Wanna hear it?" She asked and without hearing his reply she plugged the earphones in his ear

"Beautiful, right?" hearing her question, he nodded, not knowing for what he answered, the song or her face

If only circumstances were different, He thought

...

Today was the much awaited day, the Holi day

"Samaira have you checked is everything ready?" Disha asked this question again for the tenth time

"Yes bhabhi, everything is ready, no need to worry"

"And Kritika the food?"

"That is ready too" she replied

"Where are those RRR?" Samaira asked while searching for the brothers

"Getting ready upstairs" Kritika replied

"Huh, and they say we woman takes time in getting ready" Samaira said

"I never think I have said that" a voice rung throughout the hall

"I have never mentioned you specifically in my sentence, I mentioned 'they'" Samaira replied back to Rudransh

Looking in his way, she found out his other two brothers were standing behind him too

"But weren't your implications towards us" he said pointing towards him and his brothers

"Right, my dear husband understands me so much" Samaira replied, sarcastically

"Okay, okay now that everyone is ready let's take this colours and start the party, everyone has arrived outside for the party" kritika said to dissipate the brewing anger and fight among the two

----

Flashes of cameras were everywhere and so were the reporters

"Ugh, why are these reporters here" Samaira whispering, complaining to the other two ladies

"Don't you know, in every Raghuvanshi's party, there are media involved" Disha whispered to her back, while greeting the guest with the men

"It's so irritating" this time it was kritika whispering

After sometime the men went to talk to other men mainly businessmens and the ladies went to attend other ladies

Suddenly a reporter popped out of no where and Kritika shouted

"Ack-" and due to this sudden intrusion she fell down, slightly twisting her foot in the process

"Hey are you mad? Can't you see" Samaira shouted while helping kritika to stand up

"It's okay" kritika said while standing up

"I am so sorry mam, are you okay?" The reporter asked

"Yeah I am fine" kritika said ignoring the growing pain in her ankle

And then the reporter told them the real deal, from the time party started not one Raghuvanshi couple had got their photo clicked and she was here for that only

Calling their husbands, everyone stood there as a couple with a fake smile plastered onto their faces

"My feets are killing me" Disha whimpered and hearing this kritika remembered her own pain in the ankle, it's also killing her

"Bhabhi I will going to sit for sometime" saying this kritika left and soon found a chair to sit on in a little faraway place from the party, lifting her saree she removed her sandal and checked her ankle

It's bad, she thought, her ankle has already formed a bruise turning blue and purple at some place

"Here" a sudden voice startled her, and she twisted her ankle more than necessary and winced

"Oww"

"Are you small child? Can't even take care of yourself, if you are hurt then go inside the mansion" Kritika couldn't believe her ears that it was her husband speaking all this

"I didn't wanted anyone to speak about you or your Raghuvanshi family" she replied while trying to put on her sandals

Her husband's stopped her mid-air and suddenly he bent down

"What are you doing?" She asked startled

Showing her ointment, he asked with raised brows

"What do you think?"

Soon he started applying it on the bruised area, and Kritika might admit he was doing it quite carefully, unlike his cold and harsh behaviour

After applying the medicine, he even bandaged her feet

"Thank you so much" saying this kritika got up and after taking one step she was about to fall but he held her

Clicking his tongue, he took her in his arms, in a princess carry

"What are you doing? Put me down" she said hurriedly

"Really huh! Put you down, by how you are walking, you will reach the house tomorrow only"

"Hmmph" hearing his reply, Kritika sighed angrily and look the other way

Ugh, the people are staring, kritika thought embarassingly while trying to duck as much as possible

"Was it necessary to carry me infront of so many people?" Kritika asked once they were in the room

"Want to walk with a feet like this?"

"You could just have me leaned on you to walk" hearing this, Raghav went silent but then he replied

"Just sleep" and with that he went outside and soon sleep also overtook kritika

...

"You are such a jerk, Mr Ryan Raghuvanshi" a full on drunk Disha kept babbling infront of her husband who was currently taking her to bedroom after the Holi party

"Just shut up, Disha" he said

"That's what I always do after getting married here, shutting up, am I some kind of doll who will always keep quiet about everything, huh tell me" her voice raised an octave in the end

"Okay don't be quite, keep talking but atleast do it in the bedroom, why disturbing others"

"No one is getting disturbed, only your the one who is disturbed, you know what Harsh is quite good than you"

"Then why don't you call him to help you here, huh?" He said, irritated

"Are you my husband or him?" She asked him, while looking deeply into his dark brown with some orangish hues falling due to the sunset

"I told you to be quite and keep walking" he said, avoiding the ey contact

"Yeah but you are much more handsome than him_" hearing this Ryan raised an eyebrow at her like asking, really?

"_but he is less colder than you" she finished

"What did you just said?" He asked but by now Disha was already passed out due to the bhaang

Shaking his head, Ryan continued to take her to the bedroom

...

"Today was so so eventful, kritika bhabhi fell and her ankle got swelled and disha bhabhi drank bhaang somehow, and now my white saree got dirty, ughh so troublesome" Samaira kept talking to herself

"Are you talking to yourself?" Rudransh asked her while pausing his music and removing his earphones

"No talking to the ghost standing right behind you" she said, with a serious and straight face

Hearing this Rudransh got startled and immediately looked behind him

"Haha_ Rudransh really you believe in all this stuff, so hilarious" Samaira started laughing loudly, and she kept on laughing till tears spilled out from her eyes

"Okay, you are so great right, then okay, I admit I have a fear of ghost good night" and with that he slept

After Samaira changed her clothes she also slept on her side of the bed and soon sleep also got her body

...

What are these weird voices, Samaira thought once her sleep broke in the middle of the night

Voices like which can be heard in some horror movies can be heard in the room currently

It's coming from the balcony I think, don't tell me I talked about ghost that's why it's happening right now

With these thoughts, Samaira tried to wake up the man beside her

"Rudransh wake up, wake up damnit" she shook him but he didn't even buged

"God damnit he sleeps like dead" she exclaimed

Having no other choice, she got up from the bed and started walking towards the balcony

Why am I feeling like a protagonist from a horror film

Reaching the balcony, she opened the sliding door and tried to look outside

"Boo!" Looking behind unaffected by anything, Samaira faced her husband in the eyes and he looked confused

"Why didn't you get scared?" He asked and she pinched him heavily

"Oww"

"Mr Raghuvanshi, quit your childish play, like I said nothing can scare me, and just like you saw your plan failed miserably so don't look out for other chance to scare me" saying this Samaira went straight to her bed while thinking

I was scared out of my wit, but thanks to the balcony window I saw that idiot awake and ready to come behind me, and also my awesome acting

I am just amazing, aren't I

Praising herself, Samaira went to sleep and this time with no disturbance till the morning

...

[If somebody dosen't know what bhaang is then it's a drink we all drink in Holi, and it can definitely make us drunk, I have drunk it once and haven't woke up till next day and also babbled very much]

So tell me how was the chapter, after very long time featuring all three couples

Many people are saying the story is slow, but guys that's how I planned this story, and if I directly jump onto the revelation scene about the brothers then there would be no fun so please bare with me

Do vote and don't forget to leave your feedbacks and thoughts on this chapter

Note : I will be writing the revelation in chapter 30/31/32, it can be any three mentioned chapter

Signing off -

27. A trip?

THIRDPERSON

"Bhabhi!!!" A sudden shout not only woke the three couples up who were sleeping peacefully but also all the servants and maids living in the servants quarter

Disha hurriedly came downstairs to see who shouted so loudly and if something happened

Upon reaching downstairs she came across the scene of a girl ducking her face inside the fridge

Upon hearing footsteps behind her the girl looked back, hitting her head on the fridge in the process and disha immediately called out to her, shocked

"Saanvi!!"

"Bhabhi what is this, yesterday there was Holi's party and nothing is in the fridge" she complained

"You woke everybody in 6 in the morning FOR THIS" Disha shouted, bewildered

"Yeah, for me, not finding food is first world problem" she shrugged

By now everyone has came downstairs, Samaira is still half asleep and so are the other men

"Saanvi, I have meeting today and your scream woke me up so early, do you want me to like a zombie or what?" It was Rudransh who was complaining

"You don't look less than a zombie" Samaira mumbled and laughed slightly at her own joke

"Did you say something?" Rudransh asked, with a pointing glare and Samaira shook her head in no

"Okay everyone, go take a bath and freshen up and I will go and do the same and then come downstairs I want to talk about something especially to you three" Saanvi said pointing towards her brothers

...

Currently it was 7am and the one who usually woke up on 8am are sitting on the dining table and eating their breakfast

"What do you want to talk about, Saanvi?" Rudransh asked

"I want us to have a family trip" she dropped the bomb and everyone stopped eating

"Now it's not such a big deal, I just want all of us to have some fun, that's it"

"And where do you want us to go?" Raghav inquired

"Hawaii" saanvi answered

"And what about Maa and Dadi? Won't they come with us?" Ryan asked while taking a bite of his egg

"Yeah and then spoil my bhabhis mood, let it be no need to call maa she always creates fuss only nothing else and for dadi, she won't say anything but seeing others in bikini and swimsuit will definitely make her uncomfortable

And anyways, dadi is on a trip with her friends, she had gone to Kashi Vishwanath temple and maa is busy doing parties with her own friends"

"And how long do you want this trip to be?" Rudransh asked

"2 week"

"2 weeks? It's too long, how will we do the work?" Raghav asked

"Simple, take your laptops and do the works there and anyways don't forget you own the company" saanvi said

"Anyways Ryan Bhai I need your card, I need to shop" Saanvi said

"My card is with your bhabhi itself" he replied

"Saanvi you should have informed before itself na, we had gone to shopping just 2 days ago" kritika said

"Don't worry we are going to shope something else today" she replied

...

"Isn't it too revealing? Why don't we buy a swimsuit, the bodycon one" Disha said

"Yeah, then why are we going to the beach, let's wear a saree and let's go to the Vishwanath temple to pray" Samaira said

"Yes bhabhi we are going to the beach, its normal to wear this type of biknis" kritika said, she has no problem in wearing bikini as she has already went to beach many time with her uncle and aunt

"Okay then" Disha finally gave into their demands

Walking through the mall, something or better yet someone catched Samaira's eye

"You all go home first, I have something to do first" Samaira said to the others

"Why? Tell us what you have to do we can wait for you" Kritika said

"No, no you all go, it's gonna take me long time to handle it" And with that she convinced everyone to go home and after that she swiftly exited the mall and blended into the crowd

While walking into the crowd and certain stall catched her eye, and she quickly went to the seller and bought her product

Walking into the quite alley, where she made sure there was no CCTV camera to record what was about to happen and no other human witnesses either

Soon after checking everything, she heard loud footsteps behind her, indicating not just one but there are more than few people

Turning to face them, she smiled which soon turned into a smirk

"I was waiting for you all, suckers"

"You still have a big mouth, Samaira baby" One of the man among them said

"And you still think from your dick, I see" she retorted back

"You are so stupid, came in such a dark alley, you would have been safe if you were still crowd, now who would save you?" Another man said

"First, I chose this place myself and you should worry about your safety not mine, and second, this Samaira needs no motherfucker to save herself" she spat out and soon took out the product she bought from that stall owner

It was a sharp foldable knife, with a sharp edge and Samaira knew she would need this to deal with all these fuckers

"You are so pitiful Samaira, no body wants you by their side, not your parents not even your husband, isn't it, I saw it in the party yesterday how he was ignoring you" The first man who talked said again, yeah as all rich man came to the party yesterday, they were present too, but Samaira didn't saw them

"Right, but a person is not pitiful until he or she herself thinks so and I don't think I am pitiful, and like I said I need no one in my fucking life to survive, not a father, not a mother and not a fucking husband

And rather than worrying about me, you all should worry about yourself" she said

"Do you know that day when we came at your home? It was actually planned by your father, he deliberately left his daughter to us" hearing this Samaira closed her eyes for few seconds, that is one of her most painful days of life and now hearing the truth behind that day, Samaira isn't even fazed that her own father can do that

These five men are her father's friends, they are quite rich than her father but still a flithy bastards,

Bile still gets rised in her throat thinking of that day when these fuckers were trying to force themselves on her, but that day too she smashed their heads and ran away from the home and came back after 3 days and still got beating from her father

Thinking of her father she remembered Rudransh's words

He is not your father

"Get that bitch" hearing the man's voice Samaira came back to her present

Opening the knife, she stabbed the man in his hands who came to grab her

Taking every man down in less than 5 minutes, Samaira was soon over with her task

Wiping the blood on the man's shirt, she kept the knife back in her dress and grabbed their boss with his collar and spat out

"Never think I am weak, you already saw my strength last time isn't it, gone to hospital for two weeks, this time it's 1 month in the hospital, but next time you won't go to the hospital, I will directly send you to hell" saying this, she left but not before stabbing her heels in his chest

...

"Samaira, what happened you took so much time?" Kritika was the first one to ask her

"Yeah it's been 1 hour" Disha asked, right now all three of them were in the kitchen and saanvi was upstairs working out

"Oh nothing, I was taking a walk in the park and lost the track time" she lied, she never wants her sisters-like friends to know her dark past

"Wait what's this?" Disha pointed out the red marks on Samaira's dress, the blood marks which splashed on her dress when she stabbed those men

Thinking about them, Samaira thought whether they were dead or alive

"Samaira, I am talking to you, what are these marks?" Disha asked again and Samaira came up with a excuse

"Oh these, I drinked some raspberry juice on the way back and it got spilled and that's why it left marks"

"Oh okay, I thought it was blood, I thought you were hurt somewhere else"

"Nah, how would I get hurt, it's just juice"

I am always the one who hurts someone not who gets hurt, Samaira thought

...

Right now it was night time and all that happened was running in Samaira's mind and she just kep tossing and turning in her bed without even a wink of sleep

Turning to face her husband she lightly called out to him

"Rudransh"

As he was also not asleep he answered back

"Hmm?"

"Can I hug you?" Listening her request he was a little shocked but still opened his arms and took her in his embrace

As soon as she hugged him she thought, it's warm

"It's just one time offer, you can't avail it everyday, so enjoy it"

"Tch, bloody narcissist, I just can't sleep that's why I need it, who will come to a narcissist like you everyday" and with that Samaira soon went into a deep sleep

...

[Their sleeping posture^^^]

Tell your thoughts

My god now I am feeling proud of how I made Samaira's character

Don't forget to make my day by voting and commenting

Signing off-

28. Welcome To Hawaii

Today is the day, the Raghuvanshi family will land there selves in the colorful and lively atmosphere of the one and only Hawaii

All of the Raghuvanshi family members are currently seated in their private jet that is taking them to Hawaii

"Aah, the feeling of getting free from studies, is just awesome" Saanvi exclaimed and Rudransh patted her head, a little too hard

"Just for few weeks, then back to Dadi and your studies"

"Ughh let me enjoy, and by the way why did you bought these two idiots" she said pointing towards the extra two men sitting beside their own boss respectively

"You are making us miss two weeks of work, we need our assistant" Ryan said, and then him and his assistant again started discussing work

"Ugh, whatever, I am going to sleep" saying this, a yawn soon escaped her mouth and she soon went into the bedroom present in the jet

"Wait, I am coming too" Disha said and behind her the other two went too

The thing is, even if they were using the private jet they all got up early and now they all are tired out of hell

....

A announcement from the pilot waked up all the ladies sleeping on the king sized bed of the private jet

"Everyone wake up and come back to your seats, we are landing soon" Rudransh bursted into the room and woke everybody up

"No need to shout Bhai, we are certainly not deaf" Saanvi said

"Whatever just come out" and with that he left

....

"It's truly beautiful" Samaira exclaimed, looking outside the window

"Isn't it, it's good to change your scenery once in a while" Saanvi exclaimed

"Yup" the route from the airport to the hotel they have booked for staying was just 15 minutes far and very soon they reached their staying place

Standing in the lobby, the three brothers went to take their keys for their room

"Here is they key to your room, Saanvi and, and here is your key, Yuvraj and Rajveer" Yuvraj and Rajveer were Ryan and Rudransh's assistant respectively

"Okay then I am going, very tired, gotta get my beauty sleep and tomorrow everyone will meet here in this lobby only" Saanvi said

"Tired? From what? Sleeping on the plane" Samaira asked and Saanvi pouted

"Bhabhi!!"

....

"Let's play a volleyball match!!" Right now everyone was gathered on the beach, which was booked by the brothers for whole 3 hours

"These brothers never leaves a chance to show of their huge bank balance" kritika mumbled to the other two

"And why should we play the volleyball match?" Rudransh asked

"Because I want to relish the day where you all three lost like a sore losers" Saanvi laughed

"And when did that happen?" Ryan asked

"Bhabhi do you all know, when we all four, came to the beach last time, they three lost to me even though I was alone and everyone on the beach laughed at them" Saanvi told them, and not just the three women but even their assistants started laughing

"And they all booked this beach so that no one can witness how much of losers they are" Saanvi again laughedand with that everyone broke into the fit of laughter

"Okay let's play now, shall we?" Raghav said

"This time, I won't play and neither your assistants would join but just you three and my cute bhabhis would play and I would just be a referee for this match along with these two" she said pointing towards Yuvraj and Rajveer

"But-" Disha started but Saanvi stopped her

"No buts my dear bhabhi, you can do it and don't worry-" Saanvi leaned in and brought herself closer to all the other three ladies and whispered

"They don't even know how to play it" she said and then went towards the chair provided on the beach with Yuvraj and Rajveer behind her and after settling herself, she shouted loudly

"Let the game begin"

And with that Samaira served the ball and shouted loudly

"This is for you, dear hubby"

....

The volleyball game went for one hour and both team were in a tie with the score of 14-14

"Just one more score, my bhabhis, you can do it, go for it" Saanvi cheered for sister-in-law

"You are such a biased person, Saanvi, who will cheer for your brothers" Rudransh shouted at her

"Well who will cheer for such suckers" Saanvi stuck her tongue out at him

Saanvi took out her phone and announced

"I am turning on the two minutes timer whoever wins, will get a suprise from me" and then she told Yuvraj to take out his phone and start recording the last bit of match

This time she wanted to record the faces of her brothers that they make while they will lose

Both the team kept tossing the ball effortlessly and the timer was running out and Saanvi's anxiety was reaching its top peak, seeing such a intense match

Last 30 seconds were remaining when Samaira hit the ball and nobody could hit it back and it fell on the men sides and with that the ladies won in the nick of time

"Yay!!!" Saanvi jumped and got up from the chair and ran into their arms

"You all still suck" she teased her brothers and Rudransh came on to their side and twisted Saanvi's left ear and said,

"You better shut up now"

Seeing him twist Saanvi's ear, Disha hit him on his hand and he immediately left her ear

"Rudransh she is your sister, behave" Rubbing her ears, Saanvi stuck out her tongue and quickly ducked behind Disha, seeing that he was coming again at her

"So what is our suprise?" Samaira asked Saanvi

"You all will know just be ready today evening" Saanvi smiled

"And what about us?" Raghav asked

"You all stay in your rooms and sulk for your loss" Saanvi said

Saanvi then pulled Kritika and whispered to her

"I have an extra suprise for you, but tomorrow and I know you will be very happy after seeing that"

After hearing that Kritika thought and whispered to her too,

"I too have suprise for you, and I am sure you would be very happy too" Kritika smiled

"Yay, I am very excited for tomorrow"

....

I promised a reader for double update but I couldn't do it.... So sorry dearie...

But anyways, don't forget to vote and share your view about today's upd ate...

Singing off-

29. What are you pretending for?

THIRDPERSON

Saanvi's suprise was taking them out and having a girl's day out and getting full on drunk

Well, Saanvi was the only one who got drunk, Disha didn't crink, kritika only drunk two shots of vodka and Samaira has high tolerance of drinking from before itself so she can drink as much as she want without getting drunk

After Samaira came back, she had to face another problem and that was a drunk Rudransh

How and why he got drunk would never be known to her but when she unlocked her room, Rudransh babbling incoherently was the sight she was greeted with

What he was murmuring was still unknown to her but when he pushed her onto the bed and started hovering above her was when her senses started working

Punch!! She gave him a heavy punch on his head and soon Samaira gasped due to such a heavy body heavily falling on her and she regretted knocking him out

"Hey, did you really got knocked out" Samaira shook him but he was limp

Pushing him off from herself, she went inside the washroom to change, and after coming out from the washroom, she slept soundly due to fact she partied so hard today, without bothering a person was passed out beside her due to her knock out punch

....

"Yes, who are you all?" A sudden knocking woke up kritika from her afternoon sleep

Half asleep she opened the door, only to come face to face with few women

"We have been ordered by Miss Saanvi to get you ready, Miss" one of the four answered

"Ready? For what?" She asked

"We are not allowed to disclose it mam, if you want you can ask miss Saanvi" the previous one answered

"Wait a sec" kritika went inside her room, as she was about to dial the call to Saanvi, a message popped up, and it too was stating that she sent someone to get her ready

Realising it was really Saanvi, she took the ladies standing outside inside the room and thus started her three hours of torture

....

"Finally, you are ready, mam" the hairstylist among them said

Kritika opened her eyes, and she thought

I do look nice

"Thank you so much"

And after that they left, while kritika checked the time, it was currently 6 in the evening

Remembering what kritika is about to do today, she was a little sad and a lot nervous, walking towards the closet of the hotel room

She took out everything needed for today and kept in the handbag provided by those ladies who came to doll her up

A sudden knock bought her out of her trance and she went to open the door

It was Saanvi and Disha standing there, and they two were all ready

"Can anyone tell me, what is it today?" Kritika asked, even though she had an idea what's it's about

"Bhabhi if you don't remember it, then it's okay, but first we have to bring you somewhere, come with us" Saanvi grabbed her hand and pulled her outside, while Disha blindfolded her with a satin ribbon

"Hey guys what are you doing?" Kritika asked, fully panicked

"Don't worry, we are not kidnapping you" Disha said and then they started walking along with her

....

After walking for 5 minutes, they finally stopped

"Bhabhi on the count of three, remove your blindfold, okay?" Hearing her, kritika nodded

"1"

"2"

"And 3, remove it"

After removing her blindfold, kritika was surprised with the scene that greeted her

"Happy anniversary!!!" Everyone shouted while looking at her

"Bhabhi I have one more suprise for you" Saanvi said and then pointed her to look towards her left

After looking there, kritika was in awe for sometime, but a certain thing broke every happy emotion inside her

Towards her left was, a setup stage, and there stood all three brothers, but only The Raghav Raghuvanshi had a mike in his hands

And then the music started...

Empty feeling was around meAimless life just had no meaningAnd my heart was beating slow, you came rescued my soul,You loved me back to lifeYou're the morning winter sunrise,Keep me warm in freezing cold timeYou are heaven-sent, you see?You mean the world for me, you bring me brighter skyIf I describe, this great love of mine,I would say

You're the airSo I can breathe just fine.Can't go on if you're gone away, I won't be okNo way I can survive.

Without youI can't breathe, I would dieHave I ever told how much I need you in my life?And I just long for you.

You're my oxygen,You're my oxygen,You're my oxygen,I can't live without you nowYou're my oxygen,You're my oxygen,You're my oxygen,I can't live without you now.

From the emptiness you save me, no more loneliness you free meOh you fuel my heart to beat, and make me wanna live,you bring me back to life.

If I'm to describe, this great love of mine,I would say

You're the airSo I can breathe just fine.Can't go on if you're gone away, I won't be okNo way I can survive.

Without youI can't breathe, I would dieHave I ever told how much I need you in my life?And I just long for you.

You're my oxygen,You're my oxygen,You're my oxygen,I can't live without you now.You're my oxygen,You're my oxygen,You're my oxygen,I can't live without you now.

You're the airSo I can breathe just fineCan't go on if you're gone away, I won't be okNo way I can survive.

Without youI can't breathe, I would dieHave I ever told how much I need you in my life?And I just long for you.

You're my oxygen,You're my oxygen,You're my oxygen,

You're my oxygen,You're my oxygen,You're my oxygen,

Cheers erupted from the crowd of three, consisting of Saanvi, Samaira and Disha

The Raghav came down from the stage with a gift in his hands and stood right across kritika

"Happy Anniversary, kritika"

But all of a sudden, kritika started laughing, and her laughter was resonating in the whole hall booked for today's anniversary

She kept laughing, laughing and laughing, till she fell on her knees and tears started forming in the corner of her eyes

Seeing her falling so suddenly, Disha and Samaira immediately ran towards her

"Kritika, what happened?" Disha asked worriedly

"Bhabhi? What happened to you? You didn't like our suprise?" Samaira asked

"No, I like it very much, after all it's my marriage anniversary, isn't it?" Kritika looked at raghav while wiping her tears

"Then why are you crying bhabhi" Saanvi asked

"No Saanvi, do not call me that, that word bhabhi, I hate it, I hate everything fucking thing which makes me remember this cruel bastard and my relationship with him" Kritika shouted while standing up

"Kritika"

"Why are you shouting Mr Raghuvanshi, aren't I right? Aren't you and your brothers just cruel bastard who dosen't care about anything or anyone, just tell me"

"What are you saying?" He asked

"What are you pretending for and being so innocent? Still don't want yours and your brothers true self to be revealed? Oh right, your sister standing here isn't, that's why, am I right?" Kritika asked mockingly

Then she turned to Saanvi and smiled at her while Saanvi was totally confused with the turns of events

"Yesterday Saanvi, I told you, that you will like my gift but I am sorry to say this, this gift of mine is going to hurt you very much"

....

Oh my gosh!!!

The singing scene was the most cringey scene I have ever written, I swear

If it's Rudransh or even Ryan who would have done it, I wouldn't have got so much cringe, but raghav I just couldn't imagine

And yes next chapter is the most awaited one!!!! Do not miss it

(Early update as I can't update on Monday,

If some of you don't know I have made a schedule for this one, update on every Monday

It would have started from next week, but gave an early update)

Signing off -

30. The Revelation Of Truth

THIRDPERSON

"Bha- what are you saying?" Samaira didn't wanted to make kritika more angry, as she was already turning red due to her current anger

"If you don't like anything in her then say it na? It was all my plan, the singing, raghav bhai giving gift, I forced him to do it, if you are angry please tell me" Saanvi said

"Everything is wrong here, not just this anniversary party but also this bloody namesake marriage of mine with your brother,

He ruined my life, not only him but both of his brothers too destroyed my sisters today" yes sisters, kritika admits now, even though they don't share the same blood, she admits they are her soul sisters, the only one who truly understands her

"Kritika, say everything clearly, what are you trying to say"

"I will Disha di, but first let's ask your husband, oh my bad, soon-to-be ex husband"

Kritika walked towards Ryan who was standing there motionless

"So, Mr great Ryan Raghuvanshi, the great businessman, the outstanding manipulator and rude, ruthless and cold man, would you care to tell us how you and your brothers managed to manipulate our life situations and make us marry you?" Kritika smiled, tauntingly

Seeing her asking, Ryan couldn't bring himself to answer her and could only stare at her

"What happened no answer? Ahh!! I understand, you probably never thought that I will understand your plan isn't it? Let it be, let me ask your brothers the same question" she turned around to face the other two remaining brothers

"Who would like to answer? Raghav you or Rudransh?"

After her question, no voice resonated in the hall, and everything was pin drop silence

"Oh, I should record this scene, the great and sharp tongued Raghuvanshi brothers are actually tongue tied" Kritika said, sarcastically

"Kritika, now you are scaring me, tell me what happened" Disha cried

"Looks like, now you have the lost the chance I gave you, don't worry I will tell you all the whole truth, yeah"

"Disha di and samaira do you both know your fathers?" Kritika asked and they both looked confused as to why is this question asked now

"No, don't look so confused, that thing is related here, so please tell me now, do you both know your fathers?" After hearing Kritika, they both nodded

"I know my father, he is Harish Rawat" Disha said, other than her father's name she couldn't remember anything

"And mine is Jay Bhagat" samaira said and kritika clicked her tongue

"Wrong, You are wrong, Samaira, your father isn't Jay Bhagat but Veer Chopra" and that's when Rudransh's words on their honeymoon rung in Samaira's ears

"What are you saying?" Samaira asked, totally confused

"What I am saying is the truth my dear samaira, you have been deceived your whole life

And you know what, the reason I asked about your fathers was because our lives are connected, wanna know how? Let me tell you

Our fathers and our soon-to-be ex husbands father were best friends" she turned around to face the brothers and raised her perfectly shaped brows at them

"Isn't that right, Mr Raghuvanshi" then she again turned around to face the dumbfounded ladies

"You know when I came to know this truth, I was also shocked, just like you all, but now I will tell you the real meaning and reason for our marriageAre you all ready??"

"Ready or not, let's just say I can't hide this truth anymore from you all

Many years back, Mr Raghuvanshi I mean these jerks father got into an accident and our father held responsible for it due to reason being that Mr

Raghuvanshi held them for embezzlement in his company and they were angry and they killed their father"

"Isn't that right, Mr Ryan, anyways let's come to the real point, marriage with us, well what else just for revenge isn't it,

Revenge on persons who aren't even alive in this world, revenge on whom who didn't even knew anything, this is why did it, isn't it?" Kritika shouted, she wanted to cry, shout and scream but her heart and mind were totally numb and even she decided she won't let her tears fall infront of these crazy bastards

Slap!

A huge and crisp slap resonated in the hall and it was Disha who did it and just didn't stopped on Ryan but she did the same to the other two too

"You flithy bastards, arrogant jerks, idiots, why did you do it, what did you get from it, you didn't get anything from it but you took everything from us, you bastards" she shouted and fell onto the floor with a thud and sobbed loudly

"Disha Di, you shouldn't have just stopped at a slap but should have also did this-" saying this Samaira kneed Rudransh in the crotch and he fell on to floor crying loudly, more loudly than Disha

Then she gave two punches to the brothers in the guts

"-and that's what you do to deceiver like them"

Kritika went towards Raghav and held his collar in her hand in a tight grasp

"You know what Mr Raghav, at first I thought I love you, I know somewhere in my heart I still do but now I won't let that shit of a excuse love control me ever again because after you the thing I would hate the most in this world will always be this bullshit of love, and if you didn't get it at first then let me tell you

I F*CKING HATE YOU RAGHAV RAGHUVANSHI"

Then she pushed him away, leaving his collar and went to pick up the long dumped handbag from the floor

Opening the zip, she took out the things that she would need the most for today

"You gave me a gift today raghav, though I know it's chosen by Saanvi as why would you waste your time on shits like this isn't it, let it be, I also bought a gift for you, two gifts actually"

"Gift no 1, I know the person you want to meet the most is your.. ugh what is the name, yeah, chipmunk right, then worry not, one of the reason for which you gave me such a hell of a marriage, that chipmunk is alive and safe and sound

Well I think that's because of me, the girl you held responsible for your chipmunk's death, I have the sent the address to you where you can find her"

"Now let's come to gift no 2,-" she again walked towards the three brothers

And threw the papers at them,

"Actually this gift is for all of you, Raghav didn't you wanted this gift so badly that you prepared on the day when we got married, don't worry I renewed it for you and not just for you but your brothers as well"

"Just sign it and give it back to us, we will do the rest" Kritika said

"But how do you know everything?" The first thing that Ryan said

"Oh you still have your voice, I thought you went dumb and deaf, as for your question, tell your brother Raghav, if he want to have some love for anyone else other than his wife he should be more discreet, like changing his screen wallpaper, and tell your brother Rudransh if he wants to have a diary then keep it in secret place, and rest there is nothing a PI couldn't do" Saying this kritika took the diary and threw it infront of them

"And yeah don't forget to sign those papers, and I just hope you all to see never" saying this kritika went towards Samaira who was helping Disha stand up

Disha stood up and went towards Ryan, wobbling throughout the way

She also grabbed his collar like kritika did to Raghav

"You are the worst man ever Ryan Raghuvanshi, and you know what from this day onwards I hate you so much, I know I shouldn't cry on a man like you but what to do my eyes are not cooperating with my heart and eyes anymore, but I just want you to know

YOU ARE THE WORST PERSON EVER"

Saying this, she left Ryan's collar and went outside the hall, with Samaira and Kritika running behind her

Here, Saanvi just couldn't do anything other than crying and thinking,

How can her brothers do it?

"I hate you Bhai, you all are the worst, I hope you never be happy, you all are jerks" after that she too ran out to find her sisters-in-laws leaving behind her brothers

....

Ohhhh!!! Finally it's done and over, I haven't told their fathers story here yet but it would be explained further so don't think your author is lazy

Share your opinions and not to forget votes,

Kritika was totally lit today, and so was samaira isn't it??

Don't forget to share your feedback

Signing off -

31. A New Life

THIRDPERSON

As Saanvi ran outside, she noticed it rain pouring too heavily that nothing can seen in sight, even in such a heavy rain, she didn't stopped searching for them

But before she could even step out, she was pulled back by her brothers

"Are you mad Saanvi? Don't you see how heavily it's raining, do you want to get sick or something?" Rudransh screamed

"Yeah! It's better if I get sick and get away from crazy selves like you three, and what concern are you showing now, huh! If the concern that you are showing me today, if even percent of that you would have shown to them na, then this wouldn't have happened today" she screamed

"Saanvi, behave yourself! Don't forget to whom you are talking" Raghav screamed

"Yeah I do know whom I am talking to, those egoistical jerks whom I have called brothers from last 20 years, who don't see anything or anyone infront of themselves and I am talking to the one who has manipulated three girls just for thir own f*cking dumb and shitty reasons" Saanvi shouted, now she really didn't care about her language and her tone

"Saanvi" the hand raised at her by Ryan stopped in the middle

Seeing her brother raising his Han at her, Saanvi sobbed and shouted,

"Why did you stopped huh? Hit me come on, after all this is not the worst you can do is it?"

"You all are worst than a monster and I hate you all"

6 months later...

It's been six months since that night happened

Six months was a lot, for the girls especially when along with them they also have Disha's two brothers to handle

In these six months many things happened, the one most painful was Disha's mother demise, and the worst was that she died just after one week of that incident in Maldives

Her mother due to inconvenience of money sold her house to someone else and now her brothers also live with them

"Sankalp and Hritik, come and have your breakfast, you have to leave for school soon" Samaira shouted, at the brothers who were currently fussing up while getting ready

"Guys, come down right now" Kritika said, then she took a bread and started buttering it for them and started keeping in their plates

Loud footsteps entered their ears and catched their attention

Once they were downstairs, Disha also came downstairs from her room fully dressed up for her work

Currently Disha has her own bakery, all of them has partnership in that bakery but Disha is the one who mostly handles it

Kritika has currently opened a art studio, where she teaches students arts and she too is doing well for herself

And Samaira, well she has opened a self defence classes for girls and currently she is working in films side by side

The investment they did by buying those jwellery really proved to be right, in the divorce, they took all the jwellery they bought with them, and it really helped them a lot

Now they are living a good life with so many sources of living and in a 4bhk home, that they bought themselves by their money

"Okay has everyone ate? Let's go today I will drop everyone to their destination" Samaira said

"How? On your bike?" Kritika asked

"Nope, in Disha di's car" she smiled cheekily

"Okay enough let's go" Disha said

....

"Wait!" Hritik shouted and due to his voice samaira haulted the car, which threw everyone sitting in the car forward, and samaira screeched

"Hritik, you stupid idiot, what happened" samaira shouted once everyone got stable

"Gosh you scared me!" Kritika shouted at him

"I think I forgot my science project" he said and everybody looked at him like asking

Are you serious?

"Guys, don't look at me like that, Samaira di reverse the car, it's very important day today and I need it" he pleaded

"Ugh, what the heck, you both go to school, I will bring it back by your lunch break" kritika said

"Okay di, love you" Hritik gave her a fly kiss, Disha and Samaira who were sitting in the front rolled their eyes

"Okay let's rock 'n' roll" samaira screamed and then started the car again

....

Today is a hectic day for the cafe, more people are coming than the usual,

All three women were sitting in a private booth, where all the customer coming in and going out in the cafe can be seen

"Disha di what are we going to do about that thing?" Samaira asked

"Yes how and when are we going to do that plan?" Kritika asked, tensed could be the thing that could describe the atmosphere among them

"Even I don't know, but we need to do that and that too very soon, but those brothers can be problem for us" Disha said

"Ugh! Those brothers again, I swear to god those motherf-" samaira started

"Okay, okay enough, let's focus on the main point here" kritika calmed her down

As Samaira was observing the customers from the sidelines, a certain someone caught her eyes, and after confirming it was the same person she became wide eyes

"Talk of the devils and the devils are here" she whispered and that made the other two confused

"What?"

"See for yourself" she pushed them both towards the one way glass panel and when they both noticed what she saw and their eyes became even bigger than her

"What the heck, for shit sakes, why this cafe of all" kritika cursed

"Talk about luck" Disha sighed

"Now that they have entered we can't throw them out but we can definitely have fun" she smirked

"What is your mind cooking now? Your smile says it's something mischievous, make sure not to damage the cafe reputation" Disha laughed

"Don't worry it's nothing harmful, and anyways today is Friday isn't it that means, its the singing day for kritika di, come here I will tell you what to do"

On every Friday, there is singing day for kritika, yeah she often sings in the cafe, and that is usually the reason why the cafe is mostly full on Fridays

After hearing Samaira's suggestion, all three of them busted out laughing

"I am telling you everyone would love this" Samaira laughed

....

So how was it?? Enjoyed it??

I am sure you would enjoy the next chapter more...

Any idea what the girls were talking about??

And do you all know, at first I wanted to make them very powerful ladies in business (like the girls who become ceo or something) but then I thought it would be too unrealistic in just six months

Next update is coming in few minutes...

Signing off -

....

32. Just a dog screeching

The thing is, what Samaira suggested is, to for kritika to play a very different song from what they usually play in their cafe

Their usual music genre would always be soft, romantic or very pleasant to hear

But the song she suggested was very different and total opposite of it, upbeat, a song about breakup but still very funny and related to their situation

Getting on the usual spot where she usually sings, kritika started setting up her mike and tuning her guitar while smiling at her sisters who were watching her from the second floor

Even though it was one way panel, she knew they were watching her

After she was done with everything, she looked at the audience to see their attention was already at her

The thing was, nobody can see her face, actually not just hers but her sisters too, nobody had seen their face in this cafe, even their employees, Sankalp and Hritik were the one who hired them

Even now basically the whole cafe was in dark and the only spotlights was on the audience

Walking near the mike, kritika coughed then started saying

"Good evening everyone, as everyone knows today is Friday and Friday for this cafe is, singing Fridays, and I am very grateful for everyone who has came into this cafe, and if you are regular customers especially on Friday you might know our music genre, but today we are going to change somethings and I hope you like it"

And then it started..

[A/n : I won't copy the lyrics from google as it would take too much place]

https://www.youtube.com/watch?v=aoxLbhCmFaA

https://www.youtube.com/watch?v=rQZJsOSw1pU

"These two songs were dedicated to the person in your life who doesn't know your values, just let go of the assh*les girl, and never lower your worth for someone else-" saying this her eyes landed on their table while connecting eyes with all of them

"-because in some time of life, I have been there, the next two songs that I am going to play are dedicated to my beautiful ladies, always stay strong and slay it!"

https://www.youtube.com/watch?v=2tJjplMngFE

https://www.youtube.com/watch?v=sY3rIlrTTh8

"

I really hope you enjoyed today's show, if yes then don't forget to drop your feedbacks in the feedback provided right the entrance, thank you all" saying this kritika exited the stage and directly went upstairs

Upon reaching the room where the other two were waiting for her, the other took her in a bear hug

"Wow di! You really slayed it there" Samaira said

"Okay, okay easy there, its my daily job, and it's 6 now, we have to pick the boys up" she said

"Guys wait here, I need to pee" Disha said and after saying that she exited the room without waiting for their response

Reaching the washroom, Disha ran into one of the empty stalls and immediately started releasing her full bladder

Signing in the relief, she zipped up her jeans and then came cut of the stall to wash her hands

As she was washing her hands while keeping her head down, a sudden clicking sound made her head turn upwards immediately and look into the mirror

Upon seeing the man who entered women washroom, a sly smirk came onto her face

"Finally you graced my poor self with your presence, Mr Raghuvanshi" Disha smirked

....

Due to Disha being gone so long, kritika and Samaira decided to check on her and thus they started their journey to the ladies washroom present in the cafe

Upon reaching there they heard-

"Somebody is groaning in there, isn't it?" Kritika asked Samaira, fully confused

"Don't tell me Disha di is doing that inside"

"What?" Kritika asked

She leaned in to her ears and whispered,

"Having sex" hearing her kritika gasped aloud hearing that and stared at her wide eyed

"What the heck are you saying, Samaira"

"I was just saying what I am thinking, anyway why do you think a man is groaning inside a women washroom, but I can't understand one thing why we can't we hear a moan, looks like that man is terrible at what he is doing" as soon as she said that, the washroom door swung open and walked out Disha, with her black heels clicking on the marble tiles

Upon seeing her face they noticed her face was actually flushed red

"Di were you alright in there?" Kritika asked cautiously

"Yeah, why?"

"Actually we heard a man inside the washroom that's why" Samaira said

"Oh it's nothing, just a dog screeching" Disha smiled, in a way that both received the message not to ask further

"Oh okay then, let's go and pick our brothers up" Samaira said

Looking back, Disha could clearly see that shameless man watching her, still not feeling satisfied after what she did in the washroom, she held her hand in the air, making sure he was watching, and flipped her middle finger

....

Today was like any other day for all the five members of the small family consisting of Disha, Kritika, samaira, Sankalp and Hritik

Right now, they all were settled on the dining chairs to have the last meal of the day

"Hritik, how did your project go today?" Samaira said striking a conversation

"It went good I got an A+" he said

"Then you shouldn't say it went good, it's definitely outstanding" Kritika said, enthusiastically

"Thanks di"

"And how about you Sankalp, today was your maths test isn't it" Disha asked and Sankalp smiled cheekily

"That di..." He stopped in mid trying how to tell her sister that he failed his test

"You failed isn't it?" Samaira asked while chewing on her food

"Huh? How did you know" he asked shocked

"I know many things, my child now isn't it your second time now, failing the test?" She said

Hearing this, everything became silent in the dining room and only moving of cutlery can be heard

"You would be grounded for two months for Sankalp, no phone, no going out and having fun, you will just go to school and come back with us, understood?" Disha warned and he nodded

"Sankalp, do understand, your all three sisters are working hard to raise you both as well as themselves, so please study hard, okay my baby?" Kritika, the most calm and loving among them said and hearing her he nodded immediately

After that the dinner went on smoothly and harmoniously and today Disha was the one who will do the dishes

After she was done with the dishes, she went upstairs to her room and started preparing for her night routine

Washing her face, brushing her teeths, she was ready for the last thing and that was changing her clothes in to the night dress

As she was taking out her night dress, a certain diary fell out from her closet and landed on the marble floor with a thud creating a huge noise

Picking up the diary, Disha sighed tiredly

This was the diary, that changed her and the other two ladies life completely

This was the thing which solved their doubts but entangled them too

But she is sure that this is something that can link to the proof of their fathers being innocent

And they will surely prove it

....

So how was it??

Share your thoughts, and don't forget to vote

I completed my promise of double update and before you comment and ask for another update here is when I will update next-

When this book will reach 95k

Signing off -

33. You are a piece of shit

THIRDPERSON

Disha was currently sitting in one of the luxurious restaurant famous for its two Michelin star and a grade food, especially the Indian food

She had no interest in coming here, but she was obliged to do so, cause she had a meeting

Today she went with a simple attire consisting of a white tshirt, a white knotting shorts with black stripes and a light pink coat to top it all

Sitting there with her shades on her eyes, she checked her watch for the fifth time

As she raised her head from the watch, she saw the man coming through the door of the restaurant through her booth window

"Ahh, finally he arrived" she sighed, and after few minutes, the man she was waiting entered

"Finally, you arrived, I didn't knew businessman like you can be late too Mr Ryan"

"I had some errands to run" he replied nonchalantly

Nodding her head in answer, she motioned him to sit

Once he was seated, she motioned the waiter to bring the food

"I had already ordered, hope you don't mind"

"Why have you called me today?" He asked

"I see, nothing has changed in you, still that businessman like stone face and straight to the point, impressive" she said, not at all amused

"Let me come straight to the point then, I need your help"

"In?" Ryan knew for a fact many things have changed between them, the incident happened yesterday in the washroom told him enough, so he was curious why she needed his help and what for

"Have some patience Mr Raghuvanshi, let's have some food first, we can talk later isn't it?" Disha smiled and on the cue the waiter entered with their order and started placing everything in order

"Let's dig in shall we?"

———————

Today it was kritika who was sitting in the cafe alone, she runs her studio only on week days, as today is Sunday it's her holiday from the studio

Today the cafe was nearly full, but due to the efficient workers everything was running smoothly, and kritika was sitting in her usual seat, where the three of them always get themselves seated, while having a cup of cold coffee and looking everything happening in their cafe

Ding!

A sound resonated in the room, indicating someone has entered their private room, kritika knew who has entered the room and her already cold face went 10 times colder

Getting up, she greeted the one whom she herself gave permission to enter their private room

"Hello, Mr Raghuvanshi" kritika smiled, a very cold and indifferent smile

"Please have a seat" if today her Disha di wouldn't request her and Samaira to talk with these brothers then she would have never called him here

"Lucky please bring another cup of cold coffee" kritika told lucky, a em-ployee of their cafe, through the intercom

"I am sure you must be confused as to why I have called you here, then don't worry I will tell you the whole thing"

"Then please start"

"I see nothing has changed, you are still that same old piece of shit, always ordering everyone around" kritika smirked

"Well then let's not waste any more time, the reason I have called you here for..."

....

"Mam today Ritesh uncle is absent, how will we practice" Tina, a student in Samaira's self defence class questioned Samaira

Ritesh is their kind of dummy to practice their self defence technique on

Today she herself gave him a holiday, because today someone else is going to be her prey, she smirked inside but maintained a calm composure outside

"Don't worry Tina, a new person is coming instead of him, and me and you both will enjoy it lot, that I can promise you" saying this Samaira rubbed her head lovingly, afterall Tina was just 14 years, one of the youngest in their class

Screeching of tires from outside broke the smile on Samaira's face and her face took a 180° turn, with a full serious mode

Clicking of the metal doors was what made every student of the class turn their head in the direction except Samaira

She could hear all the students gasp, and hearing them made Samaira scoff, what's so good in him to make everyone gasp, just good outside and inside full rotten, this was what Samaira was thinking

"Is this where Samaira teaches?" She heard him asking and right on the cue she turned around with a fake smile

"Yes Mr Raghuvanshi, this is where I teach"

"You do know we have to talk, right?"

"Yes, I do know, but before that I need your help with something" Samaira said

"With what?"

"Come here" and that's the moment Rudransh regretted the most, ever agreeing to it

"Ugh, it fucking hurts, you hit like a man" Rudransh groaned

Hearing him say that, made Samaira hit on the same spot where he was hurt the most and he screamed out loud

"Just remember, that this pain was inflicted on you by a woman, and I am better off as a woman, like I always say, I don't need a man and I don't want to be a man too"

"Leave all of that aside, what's the matter, why did you called me here?"

"You really eager isn't it?" Samaira laughed

"Yes, I am, to know what's the thing that you three called us brothers" Rudransh said

"The thing is..."

....

Darkness...

That was the thing surrounding the brothers not from today but from a very long time, it has been their companion for as long as they can remember

Currently they were sitting in the living room, surrounded by that very own darkness, from within as well as from the outside without any ounce of light entering the living room

Each one of them lost in their own thoughts and questions, everything revolving about their life and decisions, all the things they did in life and weather it was good or bad

But in some way or other their thoughts were yet connected with each other

"What should we do about today?"Rudransh decided to break the ice

"Should we help them?" Raghav turned towards his elder brother

"Yes we will, cause this is the least we can do for them after what we did, and if what they are saying the truth, then I am going to kill that man with my very own hands" Ryan's eyes were bloodshot while his hands were tight in a fist with veins popping from it

If.. only if what they were saying is true then soon it would be your last day, all the brothers had only one thing in their mind

....

See your author is loyal, as soon as 95k target was completed, I updated

Thank you so much for all the support, we are just 5k away from a huge milestone

So don't forget to vote and tell me about today's update

Signing off -

34. Execution Of Plan

[Always remember when the girls talk among themselves and mention
Mr Raghuvanshi they are talking about the guys father]

THIRDPERSON

"Fucking."

"Bastards."

"Always."

"Make."

"My."

"Blood."

"Boil."

Disha was the one cursing out freely and she cursing none other than the
famous Raghuvanshi brothers while doing her gun shooting practice and
hitting bullseye everytime

"Woah! Looks like someone is in a bad mood huh" a voice rung in the sing song voice in the training arena

"Fuck off, I am not in the mood right now" she told that person off, her tone angry and rude

"And now that's not how you speak to your best friend is it, my dear Disha" the man laughed

"Harsh, stop getting on my nerves, just leave or else instead of this dummies you would be my target" Disha threatened him

"Ahh! You are so scary, but I don't fear you so just tell me what happened, you aren't angry for no reason" he said, while leaning onto the wall, his hands crossed

"You won't leave until I tell you right? Then fine here is what happened"

And then she started narrating something that happened in the past few hours

Disha was currently doing her daily exercise, that included her running for straight one hour and some muscle streching

Beep!

A notification went off and she took out her phone to check who messaged her in 6 in the morning

Seeing the person who messaged her, her mouth was curled downwards with unhappiness

The message reads -

Meet me at the cafe xxx right now, I have what you needed

Even though, that man's number wasn't saved in her new mobile, she knew only three men in her life who loved to order around

Those three brothers..

Sending a quick reply, she went home jogging

Walking inside with the spare key she keeps under the pot of the money plant, she came face to face with her new maid, actually there is two of them whom she hired

They were duo of mother and daughter, who were wandering on the street, and they begged them to hire them

Pitying them Disha hired them, and now it's been one week since they are here

Not minding her, Disha went upstairs, and took her sweet time to get ready

For today she took her fav white sleeveless crop top pairing it with again her favourite knee length skirt with a high slit, as for the jwellery she went with hoop earrings and some bracelet along with a watch

Walking downstairs, she took a pair of white heels with lace tying it up to her knees as she was wearing skirt today

Checking the time, it was currently 7, she really took her time getting ready, she thought to herself

Leaving the house, she unlocked her car, sat inside and drove away

The cafe he chose was far away from her locality, and it took her 45 minutes to reach there

Walking inside, Disha felt that the cafe's atmosphere was more urbanic and modernized, but still friendly

He has already told he had booked a table for them, so she asked the person near the counter and he directed her the direction

Ryan actually booked the place with the best view and it was a private room on the second floor of the cafe

"I didn't knew the person who is in need will also be so late, Ms Khurana" Ryan said in a taunting voice

[A/n : Khurana is Disha's maiden surname]

"What can I do Mr Raghuvanshi, it's just I am a woman, I take my sweet time to get ready you know, and if a businessman like you can be late, then why not a measly woman like me" Disha smiled, in the same taunting way, while sitting on the chair kept opposite to Ryan

"Anyways, here is the information you needed, can you tell me now what you didn't wanted to look in my own father's case?"

"Because, if you wanted you could have done it way back, but like a useless person you and your brothers are, you didn't but chose to blame my and my sisters fathers so nope not giving it to you,

And by the way is this information accurate?"

"Yes"

"Thank you very much" Saying this Disha got up, as she took few steps, she turned around again and walked where Ryan was sitting

When she was standing just few centimetres away from him, she leaned towards him, till her lips were brushing against his ears,

"Last time I forgot to tell you this, don't be a pervert and enter a ladies washroom, because I just hit you once, other ladies will break your legs" then Disha moved a little back, and now their face was few centimetres away

Holding his tie, she tightened it and smiled while asking,

"Alright?" And with that Disha left for good

"By what you just told me, wasn't it you who did all this to him, how come you are irritated right now?" Harsh asked

"Just their names are enough to make me irritated, now get lost or I would really make you make target" realising she wasn't kidding, harsh quietly slipped away

All this while Disha was only thinking,

It's time to execute the plan..

"Di, did you get that?" Kritika asked Disha

Currently they all were in the secret room that is located in their garage, it's the place where they always come to plan, cause you never know where your enemies are..

"Yes, here is it"

Samaira took the envelope and ripped it open, the things inside it was photos of three person

And behind each photo, it was their personal information

Samaira took one photo, and took one pin and secured it to the soft board on the wall

"His name Jayprakash Shukla, a former businessman, one of our suspects for the murder, as he had a rivalry with Mr Raghuvanshi"

"Next is Umesh Yadav, another rival of mr Raghuvanshi, they are actually life long rival, so a stronger suspect"

"And last one, Ramprakash Vajpayee, A past worker in Mr Raghuvanshi company, he had gone to jail because of him, so he has a strong motive"

"But to prove any one of them is the murderer we need the proof, and how would we gather it?" Kritika asked

"We will, just wait and see" Samaira smirked and then started narrating her plan to gather proof

....

First of all thank you so much for 100k on this book,my first huge milestone

Next, if anyone of you didn't know, two more chapters are coming after this

Thirdly, this book now has a trailer, go check it out in the intro chapter

And lastly don't forget to vote and comment...

Signing off -

35. Pyscho

"Every girl should be able to protect herself, because you don't in what way any danger can come

In last few weeks I have taught you all many things, like how to use a gun, how to untie ropes and many other things and today we are going to learn how to free yourself from handcuffs

Yes you heard it right handcuffs, one of the most difficult things to get out of, and also one of the most painful thing to go through" Samaira stopped and looked at her each and every student

"I know everyone of you is thinking where would we use this if we are never getting in this situation, but you don't know what the life would throw at you, now do you? So the simplest trick is to pick the lock with a hairpin like this" samaira showed a live demo while locking her hands in the handcuffs and opening it with the hairpin in her hair

"Now what if your hands are behind you back, now you possibly couldn't open it with a hairpin now, can we? So what are we going to do is simple" Samaira smiled

"Simply bear some pain, dislocate your thumb-" and again samaira showed them a live demo by dowing it with her own thumb

"-like that and just simply take out your hand and relocate your thumb, ugh, yeah just like that"

"Now you should learn how to dislocate it and not break it, I will teach you all that too, and one useful tip, do not dislocate the thumb of your dominant hand, like here I did it with my left hand, so that I can take ahold of this freed handcuffs and use it as weapon for the person infront of us" Samaira said

The students were not surprised by how their teacher showed them the trick, she was always different from everyone else, she never taught what others did, her way always different and unique

Nobody would teach a 8 year old girl how to operate a gun, but she did and this year old was the youngest in their classes and she could have easily evaded teaching her to operate but she didn't

She always said to them,

'Age dosen't matters, you mind power does'

"Okay that's it for today, practice what I have taught you today, but only till your body can handle it, never exceed it" Samaira warned her students and then bid them goodbyes

"You can come inside Mr Raghuvanshi, no need to hide in a place where even a weak eyesight person can see you" Samaira exclaimed

"You really saw me!" He exclaimed

"Yes, because I am not 70 years old with a very bad eyesight, now am I?" Samaira asked sarcastically

"My bad to think you would lose your sarcasm"

"Yeah too bad, nature dosen't change"

"But what you taught your students was just-"

"-very pyscho way, I know no need to tell me" Samaira stopped him in between and completed it herself

"I was going to say unique, it looked like you had too much experience about it" Rudransh said

"Anyways, why did you brought your ugly ass here anyways"

"Ouch! I am hurt"

"OMG! I fully intended to do that" samaira said with a straight face

"Now tell me why did you came here? And don't you dare lie, I will castrate you here itself if even one lie spew from your mouth" Samaira threatened

"I will, if you tell me where did you learnt all that things"

"Hah! Like I will something so personal with a stranger who has been my husband for what, just four months" samaira exclaimed

"Your loss, I had a good reason to come here"

Samaira thought for few moments, contemplating to tell him or not, but then shrugged, and decided to tell him

"Okay fine, I learnt this all from a woman who lived in my neighborhood at the age of 12, she is one of the strongest woman I have ever met and she was my role model, one of the only woman who gave me parental vibes in my whole life" Samaira completed then looked at Rudransh while raising her her perfectly shaped brows at him

He too raised his brows at her asking her, 'what?'

"You idiot! Now tell me why you came here" Samaira said, somewhat impatient

"No reason, I was just passing by,so thought I can drop by and irritate you, like now see you are getting irritated" hearing his reply Samaira screamed loudly

"GET OUT!"

"Hello Mr Ramprakash" Kritika smiled while gracefully sitting infront of the creepy old man who was full on checking even her fully clothed breast

[Her attire]

"Why did such a beautiful lady called me here today?" Lust was dripping from old, cranky voice

"I am here to discuss something with you today" Kritika kept her fake smile intact on her face

"What is it?"

"I want to know everything that you know about the Mr Raghuvanshi case that happened 15 years ago"

Hearing the name Raghuvanshi, his face lost the colour and immediately stood up, ready to leave

Kritika knew something like this is going to happen, she took out her gun which she has just bought legally and kept it on the table

"Mr Ram, what's the hurry, I will myself escort you out once my QnA is finished with you, so please be seated or else-" Kritika pointed the gun kept at the table with her eyes

Fearing his life, as there was no one else in the place where they were sitting,

"That more like it, now will you start speaking or I know more that one ways to make you speak, you know you are so disgusting, your name is Ram, Lord Ram were a one woman man,

And you having seven affairs with girl 20 years younger than yourself, or more like you are their sugar daddy, isn't it, I have every proof against you

First you would be stripped off your non existent reputation and then I will shoot you, now start speaking" Kritika said

"I also don't know much but I will tell you everything I know"

"Did you kept your shitty mouth shut? If not my men has still kept the trigger on your family"

"I didn't tell her anything, I have kept your secret, please let my family go now" Ramprakash cried and the person on the other side said

"Your family will be off the hook, but don't you dare oversmart me" and with the other line went dead silent indicating the other person has kept the phone

Here Ramprakash wept for himself and his family, because even though he knew who the person was behind Mr Raghuvanshi's murder, he can never cross that person who is the murderer....

....

So how was it??

I am so sorry, but triple update can't be possible cause, my brother is the biggest hindrance in my writing

HE DELETED THE THIRD UPDATE WITH HIS OWN HANDS 'ACCIDENTALLY', LIKE I CAN'T EVEN SCREAM AT HIM

So don't forget to spread your love on this chap by voting and commenting

Signing off -

36. Wedding Bells

C lapping, that's what has recently surrounded kritika in the cafe

Appreciation of people and their praises are also one of those things which is included there but all this feels nothing to her, everything feels like something is missing

I miss how simple my life was before all this fiasco, how I used to find happiness in even of the tiniest things and be satisfied, but now I can't say the same about it now

"Mam somebody is asking for you" Ravi, the person who handles their cafe most of the time informed Kritika as she was busy having the rest of her day

"Who is it?"

"Somebody named Saanvi Raghuvanshi" hearing her name kritika jolted up and all the tiredness vanished from her eyes

"Send her in!!" Kritika exclaimed

After few minutes of fidgeting, Kritika heard footsteps from few steps away from the door

As soon as she heard the knock on the door, she answered, "come in"

Facing the door with a happy face, she came face to face with the only person she never hated in that Raghuvanshi family besides dadi

"Saanvi" she opened her arms, that send the message to Saanvi without any words to give her a bear hug

"I am so happy, seeing you after so many months" Kritika said

"Mee too bha-" Saanvi bit back her tongue remembering she was no longer her sister-in-law

"You have changed and in a good way" Saanvi exclaimed after breaking their long hug

Today Kritika decided to go more in sexy type of casual and seeing the little Saanvi giving her compliment, she swelled up with pride

After settling down, kritika decided to face the elephant in the room and ask why did Saanvi visited their cafe

But even before she could say something, Saanvi blurted out,

"I am getting married"

"What! Really, that's great!" Kritika exclaimed

She was truly happy for her, "who's the lucky guy?" Kritika wiggled her eyebrows at Saanvi

"Karan Kukreja" Saanvi sighed dreamily

Kritika again took her in a bear hug and whispered to her after breaking the hug

"I hope you be happy in this marriage Saanvi and don't ever end up unhappy like us, just remember whatever happens never ever sacrifice your self respect in the name of marriage like I did" kritika sighed

"I know Kritika Di" Saanvi replied

"Just wait for some time, the other two would be coming soon too"

"Di I don't understand, every clue that we are getting about Mr Raghuvanshi's death is leading to a dead end, I don't understand what to do next" Samaira groaned

Now she is regretting ever taking up the mysterious case of Mr Raghuvanshi's death, because everything is leading them nowhere

Every person they are meeting who was related to Mr Raghuvanshi is either to scared to speak for some reason or they don't know anything at all

Nothing is working who are afraid to speak, no money and no threat

"I am getting the same thing" kritika said

Even Disha, who have learnt everything related to computers couldn't get anything on the web

"I think we are missing on something, something important" Samaira said

"But we just can't put our fingers on it" kritika continued

"But what?" Disha thought

Suddenly samaira snapped her fingers like something clicked her

"That's it, I know now"

"What" Both the ladies questioned her

"We have to read Jheel aunty's diary again, I am sure we are leaving some clues there, something is related to her diary only that we can t pinpoint"

(A/n : Jheel is Disha's mother and I mentioned one diary few chapters back)

"Let's do this, we all will read the diary for atleast three times and write down everything we deem important and let's tally with each other and see what's missing out" Kritika suggested and everyone agreed

"Phew! Finally we did it, and finally everything is over" Disha exclaimed

"But it feels like we are going in circles and nothing is like it seems" Kritika sighed

"You are right my dear sis but still now we know all our question would be answered at one place and that is-"

"The Raghuvanshi mansion"

(At the Raghuvanshi mansion)

"I am so glad my three sisters decided to join me" Saanvi exclaimed with happiness after seeing Disha, kritika and Samaira at the doorway

There is 2 weeks left for the wedding but to solve the mysterious death of mr Raghuvanshi, they came at the Raghuvanshi mansion quite early compared to their other relatives

Taking them inside, the three girls had same thoughts

This house feels the same but yet so different at the same time

As Saanvi didn't knew they would be coming so soon she didn't prepare any rooms for them

"My di's, please wait here while your sister will go and prepare a special room for you three" Saanvi said

After she left, kritika was the first one to speak up

"I don't know why but I feel bad for using Saanvi's wedding as a bait to find out the truth"

"Chill Kritika, it's not like we are doing something illegal now are we, it's just that we are doing things our way" Disha said

"What are you doing your way?" A voice asked, and even before turning around everyone recognised that voice

The three girls rolled their eyes while plastering a fake smile, they turned around to face their ex mother in law

How can they forget they have to face this witch when they would visit this mansion

"Our dear ex mother in law I think what we talk about shouldn't concern you or anybody for that matter, after all there is ex infront of mother in law for a reason, isn't it" Kritika said while smiling

Hearing her response, Lalita Raghuvanshi gave a typical tv series mother in law's reaction, she screamed while the three covered their ears to minimize the damages their ears would have

"How dare you! You flithy girl"

"Dear Mrs Raghuvanshi, just so you know that you have no rights to shout at us or even raise your fingers because your sons are no longer our husbands and the insults you hauled at us before, we were stupid to take it all without any sounds but don't think we would not do something now" Disha said

"And I am quite surprised that even after what your sons did you still have that nerves to shout at us and call us flithy, now I really doubt that such a pure soul like saanvi can really be your daughter, after all you are such a bit*h, but really your bast*rd sons deserve a mother like you-" before samaira could continue, Lalita launched herself at samaira in attempt to hit her but soon a hand caught her

Kritika took hold of her hand and twisted it behind her back and kept her in place, gritting out her words for Lalita to hear her clearly

"Mrs Lalita Raghuvanshi, I would say this for the first and last time, never ever hurt my family, the girl you were about to hit is my baby sister, so I won't hesitate to hit and break your hand for the thing you were about to do and never think we are the same as before because we aren't, now we have each other and don't worry even we don't want to see your witch like face once Saanvi's wedding is done we will out from this hell house you call home" saying this kritika left her

"What the hell is going on here?" A voice came from the entrance of the home

The three girls sighed while samaira said out aloud

"The drama is about to be start bitches"

I don't know why tragedies happens in my life but I was seriously on my verge to kill my little brother

He again deleted my one full update and I had to write this one again but still I hope you enjoyed this one

Signing off-

37. Turn Me On

Guys there are something which I want to say before you proceed to read further

I know this would be a spoiler but still-

THIS BOOK WILL NOT HAVE A HAPPY ENDING BUT SURELY A SATISFYING ONE

The ending where after reading you won't be disappointed and I can assure you that..

And another is I am planning to end this book soon around 45-50 chapter max...

No back to our story...

"Oh just our luck, I sometimes feel like we live in a daily soap drama you know your timings are just perfect isn't it" Disha groaned

"You absolutely told what I wanted to say di" Kritika smiled

Turning around facing them, they came face to face with three familiar faces and one unfamiliar face, female face to be exact

"I didn't knew polyandry is famous in India too" Samaira said eyeing the girl standing between the three brothers with some vibes that said

'They are mine'

"Anyways, I don't give a flying fuck to it, where did saanvi went? Its been more than 20 minutes, and she didn't come back yet" Kritika groaned and soon she heard her footsteps, even before anyone else, and said

"Finally you are here" Kritika turned around to face the stairways where Saanvi was coming down, and smiled so wide like she wasn't frowning a few seconds back

"Oh! Who is she?" Saanvi pointed to the woman

"Vedika" Raghav said calmly

"Oh so we finally meet the bit- opps sorry the one and only chipmunk" Disha smirked

Raghav said something to her and she went inside the house and somewhere upstairs

"Aww! Rude Mr Raghav, you didn't even let us meet your dear chipmunk, not fair at all" Kritika mocked

To not let the things escalate more, Saanvi quickly jumped in and chirped happily, "Di, let's go upstairs, I have set up your room"

And with that she dragged the three of them from them but not before Samaira glaring at them and flipping both of her middle finger at the brothers

"Samaira quit it and let's go" Disha saw what she did and dragged her upstairs

"I am sorry di, I have prepared only one room for you three" Saanvi said apologetically

"No worries my dearie, it's perfect for us" Samaira said

"And it's not like we will stay here forever, now will we?" Kritika exclaimed

"You all can change, I will call when the food's done" and with that she exited

"Let's get changed into something more comfortable" Disha said

And their comfort clothes were a top and a baggy bottom

[Disha's]

[Kritika's]

[Samaira's]

While they were getting comfortable, here was Saanvi standing infront of her brothers with a glare in her eyes and frown on her pretty face

"You three might be my brothers, but those women are my soul sisters, the women I love the most in this entire world along with dadi, so mind it but I won't hesitate to hurt even my brothers if your hurt those three" She actually sounded menacing, after all she was also their sister

If she is angel then she also has a devilish side to her and she was damn serious about each and everything she said to them

"Seriously Saanvi? For them you would hurt us?" Rudransh asked

"Yeah, without a doubt" and with that she left leaving three men dumbfounded

It was currently 9:00 in the evening and the atmosphere around the dining room in the Raghuvanshi's mansion could be described in one word

AWKWARD

And Samaira had even of this awkward situation so tried to lighten the mood

"Why so serious everyone?" She laughed

"Samaira don't" kritika said

"But di the atmosphere here is killing me"

"And I miss those two monkeys (Hritik and Sankalp)"

"I miss them too, but let's just eat for now"

Everyone just watched the two interacting and with that the conversation got over along with the awkward dinner time

Kritika has developed a habit of reading before going to sleeping so while the other two went to do their own work, she went towards the library in the mansion

Opening the door, she searched through the vast and different book until a certain book catched her eye and she got it

But suddenly a hand out of nowhere and by reflexes, which were the results of practicing self defence with Samaira, she took the book in her hand and attacked the one behind her

A manly and throaty groan escaped from the person behind her and she immediately cringed

"You brothers have a habit or is this in your bloodline to evade any woman's personal space, huh?" She screamed and due to the face that the library was little empty, her voice echoed a little

"Aren't you getting two comfortable in someone's else house" he was still angry from what saanvi told them earlier

"I knew Raghuvanshi treated their daughter in laws lika a trash but even a guest like this, I never knew" Kritika said sarcastically

"I see you have became quite like a Samaira after staying with her" he remarked

"At least I got to learn something good from her, not what I learnt after staying after staying with you for almost one year"

"And what's that"

"The only thing I have learnt with staying with you is,and that is crying"

And with that she left, not in the mood to read anymore, because a certain someone already ruined that

As she was going to her room, a sudden hand wrapped itself around her and pulled her in a room

She didn't shout, she was calm because she knew she can take down any person with the self defence tricks Samaira taught to them, to her and Disha

"I should have known, it was you, dear chipmunk"

"Cut this crap, I just want to warn you, stay away from my Raghav" she threatened

"Yours? I didn't knew you objectify him but anyways what can I expect from a lover of a idiotic person

Anyways for your childish threatening, I just want to tell you, that man and his brothers just have the face and money, a lots of it, but their personality is just a big fat zero for me and my sisters

I think for you Raghav would be perfect, because your personality is just as same as him, and let me tell you a secret-" she leaned into Vedika's ear and whispered

"I won't again fall in love with a person who can't even turn me on" and with that she left with a smirk on her face..

So how was it??

I personally enjoyed writing this chapter and even more enjoyed writing a savage kritika □□□□□

What your first impression of chipm- uhmm Vedika?

She would also be an important character from here..

Don't forget to vote and comment!!!

Signing off -

38. The Engagement

Happiness was overflowing in the Raghuvanshi's mansion, reason was their only princess was getting married and it was no less than a celebration of a festival

Today was her engagement and everyone was busy, even the girls were busy and they didn't had anytime to think about the real reason they came here

They wanted everything to be perfect for their baby sister, after all even if they hated this family, dadi and Saanvi will always be the person they love the most

After dolling up Saanvi for her big day, they went to their own room to get ready, but only after making sure Saanvi was perfect

Entering their room, Disha went first because according to the other two, she has the longest routine and she should go first

And with that Disha entered the washroom and the other two started doing their makeup well mostly kritika doing both of their makeup cuz according to Samaira she sucks at this girly stuff

And finally after two hours of prepping, all three of them were ready

[Disha - Kritika - Samaira]

And with that, they went downstairs, only to come face to face with the Raghuvanshi's relatives

"Ohh look who is here" Kalyani Agnihotri, sister of Mrs Raghuvanshi and a total bitch just like her

They decided not to spoil their mood and tried to ignore, keyword being, tried

"Look at how they have dressed, it feels like its their engagement only" she snickered, and now Samaira had enough, she was about to break the bitch's face but disha beat her to it

"We dress like this because we actually have a body to show to others not like a certain someone" she said with a smirk

"And after all this curves are meant to be shown, isn't it" Kritika added

"Looks like after leaving this mansion surely got you sharp tongue" the woman said

"Surely it did, oh wait we didn't got it after leaving from here, but we surely didn't discover it before" Disha said and left from there

The Engagement party soon started and guest started crowding the area, and the to-be-groom was already waiting for his to-be-bride

And then came Saanvi, looking ethereal and totally stunning in her peach coloured gown and pretty jwellery adorning her with a even stunning smile on her face, and along with her, her brothers came down too

Soon Saanvi stood beside Karan and then began the ring exchange ceremony, everyone cheered and hooted for the newly engaged couples and by seeing their rings, everyone was in awe

After all of this, it was time for the real celebration, some dancing and singing and more lot of fun

Kritika took the mike, and many people mostly their ex relatives made some ugly faces, which kritika ignored,oh so swiftly

Not gonna spoil my mood on this dumb bitches, kritika thought

"Today is a wonderful day, my baby sister, Saanvi is engaged, it surely feels surreal and amazing and I just wish her all the happiness in her life, so today I want to sing a song dedicated to the newly engaged couple"

And then she started singing

https://www.youtube.com/watch?v=V7LwfY5U5WI

After she ended, claps erupted from the crowd, obviously those ugly bitches weren't one of those who were clapping

She was shocked even the brothers and that Vedika were clapping

Samaira and Disha soon also came near Kritika and Samaira took the microphone from Kritika

"You seem like a good man Karan, but one wrong move and if you make our baby cry, I will make sure to hit that body part of yours, that everytime you use it, you would certainly remember me and my beatings" Samaira threatened

Karan visibly gulped but soon answered back, with a smile

"I will never, even if you haven't threatened me"

"That's good" this time it was Disha

And with that, they got down from the stage and started roaming in the big ass living room of the Raghuvanshi mansion

They, Disha and Kritika, chatted with some of the ladies that were friends with them when they were the Raghuvanshi's daughter in laws, while Samaira just stood there bored

As usual, her bladder decided to be the villain and the sudden urge to pee was very much to handle for her, so she excused herself and after informing the other two, she decided to make a trip to the washroom

After emptying her bladder, she stood infront of the wash basin and washed her hand and came out of the washroom after checking and making her hair right

As she was about to enter the living room to join the other two, but something in the dark hallway caught her eyes, or more like someone caught her eyes

It was a dark figure giving something to the waitress that was serving in the party, whom Samaira has seen

And then the waitress added the thing given by the dark figure to one of the drinks that she was holding on a tray, due to fact there was only half light coming she couldn't even makeout if the dark figure was a man or a woman

Soon the waitress left, and Samaira decided to follow her, because whatever the waitress added didn't seem good to Samaira, and she could feel it

After following her, she became wide eyed once she saw giving the drink to her own sisters,

This fucking bitch!

Storming her way to the crowd, she took the drugged glass from Disha's hand and threw it on the floor, shocking everyone in the process, even the other two

Everyone became quite due to the sudden action of her and the party which was in a full swing, became dead silent

Turning around, Samaira faced the waitress and gave her a tight slap and series of gasps followed after the slap

"What are you doing, Samaira?" Disha screamed, she was shocked by her behaviour

"I am doing nothing wrong, this bitch had given a drugged drink, and you, who told you to do so? Huh, tell me who gave you that drug? Tell me" Samaira screamed crazily

She can never bear someone hurting her closed ones, more specifically those two women standing beside her, trying to calm her down

"Samaira clam down, maybe you are wrong, maybe it's not what you think" kritika said, in attempt to calm her down

"Then what's this" she showed the clip she recorded showing everyone what she saw and everyone once again gasped

"Who gave this to you?" It was Ryan this time, and the waitress knew she was in trouble

Crying and sobbing, she lifted a shaking and wobbly finger at someone and to say they were shocked, would be an understatement

The finger was raised at Vedika..

Woah! I can't believe I updated so fast

But anyways how many of expected the above scene, but is it really Vedika or someone else?

Drop your own guess in the comments and leave a vote

And before I update the next chapter, can you please complete a vote target

Vote target - 350+

I will try to post as soon as possible because I have to end this book soon too..

Signing off-

39. The Secret

Can't believe we will be completing 40 chapters in this book soon, gosh it was surely a journey with you all and can't even believe, I gonna end this book soon, mysteries will start unveiling from next chapter...

"You bloody bitch, I will kill you today" Samaira threatened as she stepped forward to strangle Vedika but Disha pulled her back

"Samaira control yourself, today is Saanvi's day do not do anything stupid" Disha said in a serious tone and hearing her, she calmed down but still cursed the lady standing in the black gown infront of her

"You are lucky today" and with that samaira left huffing and puffing in anger

The Engagement party was done and over, Kritika and Disha were also worried for Samaira and they can't even think of a person who would want to hurt them

Disha don't thinks that Vedika is the one behind this fiasco but then who is it, that she really can't pinpoint

"Hey, am I that boring that you are zoning out now while talking to me" Harsh asked

"Yes, you can be ranked the highest in the most boring person ever" Disha said back, sassily

"But really are you okay? Samaira told me what happened yesterday" Harsh asked, now concerned

Yes, Harsh has a good relation with both the other ladies and they have also told him about all the things that happened to them

Harsh also helped them a lot actually, and Samaira actually sees him as a brother

"I am fine my bestie, it's just everything that is happening is overwhelming me,but yeah I am fine" Disha smiled

"Okay then if you say so, but always keep me updated okay, don't forget to call me if anything happens anyways duty is calling me" he waved at her and then left the cafe owned by the sisters

"Yeah I will" Disha shouted at him and then leaned back into her chair comfortably

Today was a lazy day for Kritika, as today was Sunday, her art studio has a holiday and she was currently roaming in the mansion like a lost soul

Gosh I miss my sisters

Roaming here and there, she came onto the second floor, the floor which is for Raghav Raghuvanshi

Looking back and forth, and making sure no one was there, she went inside his office

Who knows I might find something here

Looking around in his office, she didn't find anything usual, looking around more carefully, she came across a bookshelf

This looks weird, don't tell me it's a secret hidden door

She tried taking out all the books from the book shelf but looks like there is no hidden door

Clicking her tongue in frustration and then her eyes landed on something which she never noticed before

A wall watch

It was hanging wall

Grabbing the lower part of it, she shook it once and-

Click

She immediately turned around and there was a drawer which was opened and Kritika immediately ran to the drawer

But what was inside it made her confused

A key?

What the heck? A key? But what for, and which door key is it?

Many questions clouded her mind and she didn't had any answers for any of them

But before she could think more, she caught a glimpse of the brothers car from the office window

Hurriedly she kept everything in place and then quickly got out of the office

Need to find out about this soon

But luck was not on her side, as she bumped into somebody, or more like the Satan himself

"What are you doing here?" He asked, he's voice mild compared to other times

"Why? Charging money just for looking around now are we?" Kritika calmed her fast beating heart and answered playfully

Sighing he just left for his room and Kritika too left like nothing ever happened in that office while just thinking about could be done to discover the truth

"Ugh, leave me" a shrill was heard in the storeroom of the Raghuvanshi mansion

Currently, Samaira had Vedika tied down to a chair and running her own head as a headache was forming due to her shrill loud cries

"Can you just shut the fuck up?" Samaira shouted and now Vedika became stunned

"Now tell me why you did that?" Samaira asked calmly

"Did what?" Vedika asked

"Why did you spiked my sister's drink and with what thing did you spiked it with?" Samaira again interacted with her very calmly

She wasn't going to let go of this matter, those two ladies matters the most in her life and she would get to the end of this matter

"I didn't do it and how many times should I say this, and why would I ever want to hurt them" Vedika asked

"Didn't you thought that we were the barriers between you and someone else, huh" Samaira said tauntingly, her voice raised

"Huh, you and your sisters coming between what, we aren't even what you think we are"

"Oh really you insensitive bitch, like I don't know, you were the so called first love of the Raghav Raghuvanshi" Samaira spat at her

"Yeah we were both each other's first love, he was mine too but not anymore because what we had was like a puppy love, a kind which comes and goes, and he fell out of it when he met her" And hearing her Samaira gasped

"You mean to say he has another woman now and he just mentally tortured my sister in this so called marriage for nothing" Samaira growled, wanting nothing more but to kill that man with her bare hands

"He didn't fall out of love today or fee months back, it happened long back, she was the most beautiful and kind girl he have ever met, like he used to say, and might say she was, anybody would fall for her but you know what I hated her because she took away something that even belonged to me in the first place, funny isn't it?" Vedika laughed

"But who is she?"

"She is....

Sorry for hanging you on cliff hanger but it would be revealed further, so please don't kill me

So do you all hate or have pity for Vedika, and what's the thought about so many secrets

Will try to update next chap soon, so try to leave you guess about what would happen next

Signing off -

40. Life Threatening

Nobody in this house knew what happened in between Samaira and Vedika

Well after knowing the woman's name, she left Vedika but not before threatening her enough for her to not lure around them for the time period they are here for Saanvi's wedding

On the other hand Kritika tried to find every possible possibility so that she could find something about the key and she knew she have to do something fast and quickly 'cuz she don't have much time left in this house

And thus she began her searching everytime the brothers would leave she would start her searching, in the whole house and it's been already third day

Kritika had made a copy of that key already so she doesn't need to go into the office again and again for the key

She tried pushing that key into every possible keyhole but nothing worked

Today was the day she would be on the third floor, till now she hasn't told this about anyone because first she wants to know about this herself and then she can inform about this to the other two

Today the she was searching in Ryan's office, but soon she clicked her tongue, totally annoyed and frustrated for not able to find anything, for still being empty handed

But as she was about to leave, a painting caught her eyes and she knew that she found something

Moving closer to that painting, she moved the painting a bit and-

Click.

She heard a opening of door from her left and she rushed towards it and peeked inside and as she was about to go inside it-

"Mam, what are you doing here" a voice startled her and she took a step back from the door

Looking at the entrance, Hina was standing there, Hina was a new maid hired by the Raghuvanshi's and Saanvi told her she is very good at work

"Oh nothing, I was just passing by, actually I was leaving only" and with that kritika left making a mental note to come back again

"These things are going out of hand" a voice echoed in the almost empty room

"What do you mean" another voice asked to the previous one

"Those girls are being pain in the ass, they are truly adamant to find out the truth"

"Anyone would be like them, because they are desperate to prove their father's innocence"

"But they are being a hindrance to us, what should we do about that?" The voice echoed

"The same thing we did with their fathers" the person smirked

Today was Saanvi's spinster party aka a day to get drunk their asses off, currently all the ladies of the house were in a well known bar

Kritika had that mysterious door in her mind and she stopped herself from drinking as she would have to be awake to know more about that door and what is it hiding or is it heading her in the wrong direction

"Kritika, my sisss!!!" Samaira slured badly and Kritika clicked her tongue because she knew her baby is drunk and down

"What happened my big baby?" Kritika asked and Samaira babbled like a baby and on the other hand Disha and saanvi were already passed out right beside her

After a few constant minutes of babbling, she also passed out right on her lap and Kritika chuckled a bit due to her overload cuteness

Kritika rolled up her sleeves, and quickly lifted all of them at once, she didn't wanted to brag but she can pull all of them at once and she is proud about it

She called one of the female waitress and asked her for support to bring the ladies outside of the club

"Thanks for the help" Kritika acknowledged the waitress and then drove off to her destination

Once reaching the mansion, she dropped off three of them all to their rooms and changed all of them into some comfortable clothes and did the same with herself

Tieing her hair in a loose bun, she poked her head out of her room and peeked in the hallway and checked the hallway and once confirming that the coast is clear she went towards her destination

Reaching Ryan's office, she opened it easily as she knew the password due the fact she cleaned all of the three brothers room herself

Reaching the hidden door easily, she again came face to face with a locked door

Taking out the copy of the key she had, she pushed it through the key hole of the door and twisted it all the while praying

Please get unlocked!!

She heard a click, and she left a huff of relief, and did a little dance for her achievement

She was about to enter the room but she heard some footsteps in the hall way, although light steps but she could still hear it

Closing the door, she quickly kept the key in her pocket once locking the door and left Ryan's office and went downstairs without letting the other person knowing anyone was even there

All of this chaotic experience made kritika a little too thirsty and that made her change the route of her room to the kitchen

Entering the kitchen she took a glass of kept in the under tap and filled it with water, and drank it once it was filled as much she wanted

As she was drinking, she felt as if somebody was watching, she felt as if someone's eyes was piercing in her back and she got that creepy vibes

Turning back, she tried to look if somebody was there through the large window present in the kitchen

The kitchen had a backyard type of area which was like a garden of the estate, and it was connected with the kitchen by a medium length window which was big enough to let a 6ft man pass through it and reach the garden

It may sound stupid but still kritika decided to inspect the garden to see it somebody was there, she was feeling like a protagonist from a horror film who was about to enter the climax of the scene

Reaching the garden, she soon started inspecting the garden, checking everything making sure everything was good and well

As she turned around, a person in black clothes and totally hid behind black mask and hat and even before she could do anything to stop that person, she was attacked by the person with a rod and she instantly

Blacked out...

I don't know where the story is going but it's ending soon, yay ending soon

So guys I am planning like a alternative ending for this book, like one with the original ending like I planned and one other ending for my readers who want the leads together

So yeah to satisfy both type of readers mine, so what are your thoughts on this, should I do it or not?? Yay or nay??

Thoughts on today's chapter, any guess as the book is ending soon who could be behind the chaos??

Do vote and comment..

Next update once we reach 200k, and it would be double or either triple update once we reach 200k

Signing off-

41. One step closer

"Why are you hurting them this wasn't a part of plan" a voice echoed and shouted

"Shut your mouth and do your work, otherwise I won't care you are related to me"

"Care to tell what are we doing here" Samaira groaned while side eyeing the woman standing beside them

Today they, the trio, saanvi and Vedika are here in one of the most luxurious and expensive mall to buy all the things and stuff, a bride could need on and after her wedding (if you know, you know)

Slightly nudging Samaira with her elbow, Disha cleared her throat and spoke up

"To help our baby saanvi for her wedding, or else why would be here"

Kritika let out a chuckle, she was currently sitting on a couch that was there in the shop of the mall, while eyeing them

She was in a lot better situation, she was currently with a bandage around her head, but still alot better

Talking about the bandage, you might be wondering what happened few weeks back isn't it, then here is what happened

After kritika was attacked by the anonymous person, she was passed out in the lawn for few minutes, 15 minutes to be exact

And that's when Raghav entered in the kitchen and noticed the unmoving figure lying in the lawn of the kitchen

Rushing through the glass door separating the kitchen and lawn, he quickly went towards the figure and once her saw who it was, a gasp escaped him

Bending down and taking kritika in his arms, he rushed through the main door not caring, he was still in his sweatpants and a vest

Driving towards the hospital at a high speed, he reached and called for a doctor for Kritika

Due to the fact that she was not hit that hardly, so there was less blood loss and she was rescued in time

After sometime, all the members got gathered in the hallway of the private floor of the hospital in which the Raghuvanshi's had 25% of shares

Kritika didn't knew, that she was attacked just few backs due to the fact that she was

One step closer

One step closer to her goal, to her and her sisters goal

She herself didn't knew the reason about the attack that's why she still now haven't told anyone about that secret door in Ryan's office

"Hey kritika" Disha shouted, and that's when kritika out of reflex slapped the shit out of Disha

"Yahh, you brat how dare you slap me" Disha shouted, shocked at her

"Oh my bad di, I was in such a deep thought and you startled me, I never meant it" Kritika replied while gently rubbing her swollen cheeks trying to soothe her

"Let it be, here take this and try it out" Disha said and Kritika got confused

"Why me? Isn't this all about Saanvi"

"It is, but she told you to try it, now don't argue with me, otherwise-" without letting Disha complete her sentence, Kritika took the clothes and dashed towards the changing room

As Kritika was getting changed, her zipper of the dress got stuck and she couldn't reach her even though how much she twisted and turned her hands into weird positions

A hand of another person suddenly came in contact with hers and startled for the second time of the day, she grabbed the hands of the person and twisted it and even herself to see who was the one behind her

"You, what are you doing here?" Kritika asked shell shocked

"Hello who's this?" Ryan answered and asked the person on the other side of the phone

"Long time no see my dear" the other person said in a sickly sweet tone

"Why have you called me" Ryan asked in a a cold voice

"No hi? Or hello? I am deeply hurt by this"

"Just state the thing you have called for, I don't have time for your bullshit" Ryan said, still cold voice

"I hope you remember I have leash of your brothers and yours in my hand, don't shout and tell me have you did, what I asked for you?"

"I would never do it, you can go and fuck yourself"

Saying this he ended the call, and huffed out huge breathe now regretting what he have done

He can't afford to do it or more like he is scared to do it

Kritika was biting her nails in anxiety, what did she mean by that, and why did she told her that

"You, what are you doing here?" Kritika shouted at the unexpected intruder

"Shh, be quite and just listen to me now" Vedika said

"I won't and get the heck out" kritika was about to shout but Vedika covered her mouth with her hand and pushed her against a wall

"What I am about to say will confuse you but please understand what you are sisters are seeing right now isn't what it seems like but what I just want to say wherever you are heading to is the right decision, because you are

One step closer to your goal"

And with that she left, leaving kritika with even bigger mystery

So.....

No need to wait anymore the whole book is published and sadly has ended scroll down to read

Signing off -

42. Truth lies behind the door

T oday was the day

Saanvi was getting married today with the perfect groom one could ever get and now she was getting ready in her room

The wedding is to be held in the Raghuvanshi's mansion itself and she was surrounded with the three woman who themselves were nowhere near to be ready

"Bhabhi it's enough, the makeup artist will do her work, you three go and get ready please" Saanvi pleaded them for the nth time

"We will baccha, but first let us take the satisfaction that we have done something for our baby" Kritika replied, with adoration for Saanvi and her face literally glowing with love

"Seeing you all is tearing me up and now I am missing my sister who is studying in Bengaluru" Sanika, the makeup artist broke their little bubble and everyone chuckled a bit

"Okay now enough you three, I want you all in your own rooms and get ready"

And that's how their baby pushed them to get ready

Today is a happy - sad day for everyone in the Raghuvanshi's mansion and for the three ladies too

Here, Kritika is anxious and truly can't wait for the wedding to be over because after that she would only be left with one day to find out the truth about the door

Soon after her inner monologue, the groom had a grand entry at the entrance of the Raghuvanshi's mansion

Dadi and Saanvi's mother were the one doing the rituals and everything for the groom

Kritika was fidgeting her finger, a habit she always did when she was anxious and nervous and Disha kept her hand above her

"Kritika, what happened?" Disha asked straightaway without hesitating because she knew something was bothering her sister

"Nothing Di, it's just I am excited about saanvi today" she replied quickly

She didn't want to worry anybody with her worries about the evidence which she herself even sure about currently

If she finds something which can prove their father's innocence, then she surely would be the first person to inform her sisters but today is not the day as she doesn't want them to spoil their moods

The groom was now settled at his chair and soon Saanvi was also walking down with her three brothers at her side and a smile adorning her lips and her beautifully dolled up with dazzling jwellery hanging off her neck and she herself draped with a purple - pinkish lehenga

She was truly happy, because it was being reflected on her face, the way she laughed while sitting beside her soon to be husband

And seeing her this happy, the three ladies who were sitting in a corner near the bar and drinking their 2nd glass of wine, were happy too

Atleast somebody is getting happiness in her marriage, they thought

Gulping her third and last glass of wine, Samaira stood from her place and went up the stage to the groom and bride with a big smile beaming on her face

And then she started, "Today surely feels surreal and I can't believe the girl I just met months back, the little munchkin and my baby boo is getting married, can't believe she is growing up-" she stopped her heartfelt speech and wiped the tears gathering in the corner of her eyes

"-But her husband to be-" she turned towards the groom and faced him with a serious face

"-Never ever break her heart or let that smile off her face because then you won't be able smile for the rest of your life, because you won't have any of you teeths left by then, and this will be my promise" she said without hesitating and then turned towards Saanvi, with a smile a lightly patted her head

"I wish you eternal happiness my boo" and with that Samaira left from there for some fresh air, because she knew she wouldn't be able to hold it any longer

Everyone were currently busy with their own business and some were sad to let go Saanvi and Kritika decided this was perfect time to find out the truth about that door

She hurried and left the room without anyone noticing, and took out the weird key kept by her in her purse for that door

Opening Ryan's office and now she she did everything swiftly, and now her hands were sweating

She was nervous and anxious, because if this door helds what she thinks it does then she will never leave who ever was behind this fiasco

Walking inside the room hidden behind the hidden door she came across a high tech locker, and she was annoyed now, how is she going to open in now

But not giving up she searched the hidden room in search of any clue and then a paper came in her notice which was too old to be here

The white paper which was turned yellowish now was now held between her fingers

She looked at the slightly torn paper carefully and tried to comprehend what's written on the paper and soon she understood that a few numbers were written on it

Trying her luck one more time she entered those numbers in the sfae lock while taking a deep breath and huffed it out when the lock clicked open

Opening the lock, she looked inside and all she found was a pen drive

She held it in her hand, and just prayed this had something, because she wanted her efforts to be payed for herself and her sisters

Closing the lock and exiting the hidden room, she made everything like it was before she entered and left and started walking towards her room, pen drive in her grasp

Entering her room, she took out her laptop and set up everything and once she opened the file, it contained the video

Seeing the video she couldn't believe what her eyes sawed and her ears heard

Taking the pen drive out, she was about to walk outside to everyone but a sudden noise of something breaking made her turn around

But even before she turned around, she was struck with a object which was enough to make her unconscious and push her into the darkness

So things are about to go down.... or up, maybe?

But tell me how's it?

43. Kidnapped

Heaviness was what Kritika feeling currently and even opening her eyes felt a big task to her

Lifting her eyelids were a huge task but forcing herself somehow she did it and regretted it as she somehow came face to face with a cheap bright light hung just above her head and making it a little difficult for her

Turning her heads sideways, she started looking around as good as she could, and immediately felt the need to puke seeing the condition of the room

Dirt was spread all across the room and there were spider webs hanging off the ceiling and sticking to the sides of the wall and there was even cockroaches and rats crawling here and there

She thanked heavens that atleast she was a cheap quality wooden bed which kept her away from those creatures and at a certain height

But she knew someone who had broke in the Raghuvanshi's mansion is certainly dangerous and after she felt some energy to move around, she tried to wiggle her hand and legs but the keyword being tried because her hands and legs were tied securely to the bedposts 'mmmhm'

This sound alerted her, as the room was shabby, it was obvious that the walls were obviously thin and one could easily hear someone from one side to another

And the person who was groaning on the other side felt familiar to her

Trying her luck, she tried calling as loud as she could without hurting her sore and cracked throat, which was not watered for God knows how many hours

"Samaira"

Immediately she heard a response which had her crying

"Kritika di, is that you?"

Now she knew along with her these bastards got her too, but the real thing was why?

"Samaira, bub how did you got here?" She again asked, her voice cracking badly

"These bastards caught me di, I saw them in the backyard and when I tried stopping them they got me" she tried explaining as nicely as she could

Few hours back....

"Why are you here?" Samaira asked the person standing behind her without even turning her back she knew it was Rudransh

"You are here for such a long time" hearing him samaira scoffed,

"Please don't sound like you care, Mr Rudransh Raghuwanshi"

"Please don't act so tough samaira, you don't always have to have such a sharp tongue while talking to me or my brothers"

"You have closed all of my options except this, being sharped tongue" she replied back still looking at the night sky but she could feel him beside her now

There was silence between them but it wasn't awkward, but rather peaceful?

"What do you need?" Samaira asked

"Today I am feeling like my sister is getting married and I feel like a rascal thinking of the past things of my marriage, like we never thought we also have a sister and we are treating a woman like that,

I know now it won't matter because what happened is now in the past, but I will just say that after this marriage I will apologize to all of you" reminiscing the past, both of their eyes got welled up with tears

"You are right, past is now past, no amount of words and sorrys can heal the wounds of this marriage" samaira said

"I know" and with that he turned her around and hugged her tightly

"I hope you three have all the happiness of the world" and with that he left

Samaira was also about to leave but then she heard something rumbling in the leaves and curiosity killed the cat but she was happy because atleast she was with her kritika di in this situation

She doesn't know why they got them, but she will surely kill these fuckers once she is out of this shitty room

Back at the Raghuvanshi's mansion

The marriage is done, and now Disha is roaming inside the mansion in hopes to find any of her sisters

Not finding them in any rooms she got tensed and decided to look for samaira who still haven't returned from the garden outside

But what she found outside made her burst into tears and sweats, there was lying shoes and some jwellery of samaira on the backdoor of the garden

She ran inside the mansion and shouted for the brothers to come down-stairs

Hearing the woman's shouts they quickly came downstairs and to their utter surprise, the woman was on her knees bawling her eyes out

Out of fear, all of them ran towards her and kneeled down, and Ryan asked her while holding her shoulder

"What happened Disha?"

"Kri- the-" because of the crying she couldn't even form a sentence

After full 4-5 minutes, she calmed down and told them the whole situation

"Don't worry, we will find them" Ryan said and got up to dial someone but at the same time, Disha's phone went off

Picking up she thought it was one of her sister and they are fine, telling her that they were pranking her, but to her utter disappointment it wasn't them but someone else

"I know where they are, just go to this address xxx"

And without wasting any time all of them went to the given address and reaching there, they all were tensed but when entering the shabby looking place they got shocked because instead of finding the two ladies in miser-able situation..

There were few men lying in their own pool of blood and after following some sound and reaching an old room, they found both the ladies with steel rod and two men tied up, and the ladies heaving heavily

And that wasn't the shocking part, the shocking part being that the boys actually recognised one man tied up..

And it was....

Next chapter would go into more detail of who called Disha and how they reached there, and would involve a little violence

Till then drop your guess in the comments

And yeah just one more chap and we would have the epilogue

#love

44. The (final) Truth

Seeing Disha and the brothers, the girls immediately ran up to them and the three of them hugged, while the brothers were thinking

Why was their own uncle tied up in this basement and why he was involved with the girls kidnapping

But their thought broke when the kritika asked

"How did you all got here?" And that brings us to....

[Few hours back]

Disha was bawling her eyes out, there was still no news of the girls, nothing was left behind the kidnappers and the brothers were still at work to find them work

Dadi and her ex mother in law went back to their other house where they lived previously in Bengaluru

The brothers contacted some top notch tracker, finders and detective

In all this mess, someone called Disha, and seeing that person calling and telling her where the other two certainly abucted girls were, she was shocked would be an understatement

But leaving everything behind, she went out in search of the other two women along with the brothers behind her

She is not going to lie, just by seeing the surroundings of the place, she was getting a bad premonition, and she just prayed in her heart that the other two were safe wherever they are

Unknown to her, the other two ladies were already taking care of everyone who dared to lay their flithy hands on them

Samaira and Kritika were already like a devil who is on a killing spree, like no they weren't killing anyone but they did enough damage to all the people who came in their way, so they couldn't get up again

Now in this entire building only one room was remaining to see who is on the inside, with light steps they went near that door and once they were close enough, they both tightly grasped the metal rod they were holding

And with a bang! they both broke through that door, at the same time and the person they saw inside shook them to core

"Rishabh uncle"

[Back to present]

"Why have you tied our uncle?" Raghav asked

"Why don't you ask him yourself?" Kritika replied

Beside Rishabh there was another person too, but they can't quite recognise him

"Uncle what were you doing here? And how are you involved in this?" Ryan asked, his voice calm, scary calm

"This women are crazy, my son get me out from here, I did nothing" he started shouting, and for one moment one can also label him as a mentally ill person or simply crazy

Seeing him like this, samaira stepped on his toes and gritted her teeth, "spit the truth otherwise..." She didn't had to complete her sentence everyone could perceive the meaning behind her incomplete sentence

"If your uncle can't start the story shall I start it?" Samaira asked but she didn't wait for any reply

"So uncle shall we start with how you killed your own brother or should we start with how jealous you were from not only your own brother but also his friends aka our fathers, or should we start with how you planned to break their friendship and create a rift between them?, Huh, answer me you old stinky piece of shit" samaira was shredding tears of anger while crushing the leg of person beneath her

They heard a loud thud, and looking behind it was Disha, who looked like she had gone in some different demension by how she was staring into nothing and her eyes seemed hollow

"Is it true?" Rudransh spoke for the first time in all this, it was in such a small voice that one could barely hear it, but right now this certain building was eerily quite, and one could even hear a pin dropping, so everyone certainly heard his question

After not getting any answer from the one who are currently being blamed, rudransh shouted, "I fucking asked you, is it true? Is it true that you are the one behind everything, is it true that you were playing us like a puppet while pushing all the blame on someone who didn't even deserved it and let us make a fool out of ourselves in the end"

Losing his cool after all this, Rishabh also shouted

"Yes it's true, I was the one behind everything, I killed your father and all these stupid girls fathers, and I am happy that I did everything" he screamed

"Why did you do that you monster, what did you got from that, you freaking devil" Disha shouted, she came out of her trance once rudransh screamed at rishabh and she couldn't keep her cool after listening to that disgusting man

"I did that because everyone loved that Harish more than me, what did he had that I didn't, and why was the one suffering would always be me, nobody ever loved me, all that everyone had with me was sympathy and pity, why is that why can nobody love me,

Everyone left me for that Harish, my mom, my dad everyone even my own girlfriend left me for him, we all were best friend but why is that after we grew up, they chose him over me, wasn't I already trying to be best that everyone, then why"

"Why did you kill our fathers then, what did they do to you?" Kritika questioned

"Who told them to follow my brothers, I will kill everyone who will be behind my brother, I can't tolerate him or anything related to him, I would have killed you all also, if you all just stayed one more day in the place where you celebrated your so called first anniversary

But you all just had to ruin my plans, but that was okay because I decided to first find the last evidence which was left by your foolish father of my crimes and you three made my work even easier, but in the end you all had to just fuck up, why is everyone always ruining my plans, and my nephews were so blind that I just showed them some fabricated lies and they even believed it" seeing him anybody could say he has gone crazy

So shifting her attention to the other person samaira eyed him up and down as if asking him what he was doing with the other person

"I am just his friend, I didn't know about any of his crime" hearing him samaira kicked him too

Suddenly a phone rang in the deadly silent atmosphere and it was the phone of Ryan which was ringing indicating someone was calling him

Seeing the caller id he picked up his phone immediately as it was his grandma calling him and listening to the other person he lost his composure and the phone slipped from his hands

"What happened?" Rudransh asked

"Mom has been arrested" he exclaimed and immediately looked at the flithy man as if asking him indirectly, why was his mom in all this

"Oh you thought I could do all of this alone, no my dear naive nephew, she was equally involved in this, actually I might say she was the one who killed your father by poisoning his food, and she was so cruel she actually added slow poison, he died so miserably and you know what's funny, the police couldn't even find the traces of poison in his body because she specially one which dissolved completely after few hours, such a nice plan isn't it" he smiled like a maniac after completing that

Soon there were police sirens heard, and the force came inside the shabby building and untied both the men and along with the police, Vedika and Harsh came too

Stopping the friend of Rishabh, Harsh cried

"Dad, I hate you, you are the worst person to support a man like this, I hope you both suffer hell in the place you are going"

Seeing him like this, everyone can put the puzzle in the place, and yes harsh was the one who called Disha as he had already overheard his father's conversation with the man beside him

In all this nobody noticed that Rishabh has stealthily removed the gun of the officer nearest to him and moved away slightly and shouted loudly

"I may have not succeeded in killing you three but today I will kill anyone of you and I don't care if I die after that, then I don't care" saying this he aimed that pistol in straight direction and

Bang!

The noise of the bullet pierced through the panicked crowd who was desperately trying to save whoever was the victim of the bullet which came out of the gun.......

So if any of you didn't remember I mentioned their uncle in chap 22 you can go back to read and applause to the one who correctly guessed that it was their mother who was behind everything

Next chap is the last one : epilogue

Everything will cleared out and this story would end

Before ending this, I might have to say that I am getting emotional so you can expect the epilogue in next week or next month atmost....

I just hope that you liked my story even if it's a little bit, or you might have not liked certain parts in the story if yes then you can certainly share your thoughts about those I am happy to hear you

Okay so don't forget to vote and comment

Signing off -

45. Epilogue.

L ongest chapter of the whole book, be ready....

The bullet was shot, and the aim was at kritika but no one would have ever thought that Vedika would be the one who would save her

Without thinking twice, she jumped infront of her and the bullet which was meant for kritika, pierced through Vedika's body and painting her white kurta with the red blood

She first fell on her knees and as if out of reflex kritika caught her in her arms

"Why?" She questioned lightly

Vedika weakly lifted her hand and touched Kritika's shoulder and spoke slowly

"I am sorry for everything" saying this she fell unconscious and an ambulance was called there to take her to the hospital as soon as possible, and save her life

The police took the other two men to their destination, and that was behind the bars

Everyone was so overwhelmed with everything that they never thought deeply of Vedika's last words and by the time they all reached their home, they were called to the hospital and the doctor broke the news that Vedika is no more

Everyone was sad, but it was an understatement they were drained with everything that happened to them in just a span of one day

The girls decided to go to their own apartment to their brothers

They packed their clothes from the mansion and were ready to leave, reaching the main hall of the mansion, the three of them stopped after seeing the haggard looking brothers sitting on the couch

After seeing them, the girls felt like the brothers have aged 5 years in one day and Disha took a deep breath and went towards them standing just before them and once her shoe came in their line of view, they all raised their heads in sync

"Aren't you going to hit us?" Ryan asked, his eyes was motionless and they were glued on Disha

Disha sighed, then she silently went to the coffee table, filled three glass of water, kept them on a tray and took them towards the brothers

Seeing her silent actions, everyone was bewildered, they all thought that what is she doing

The brothers silently took the water from her while she sat on her knees to come face to face with them

"I won't hit you or blame you'll for blindly trusting your uncle who wanted to push all of his blame on our fathers and us, I won't scream or shout, I won't do any of that because I am tired of everything, this drama, this everyday bickering and fighting and I am exhausted

I need a rest from everything, everything has a breaking point and I guess everything that happened was my breaking point, I sometimes feel sad that I am not strong like samaira or someone like kritika who can handle herself emotionally and mentally-" she stopped herself from crying, she has cried enough time in this mansion, not anymore

By now kritika and samaira has also joined her on the floor, while holding her shoulders on either side

"-I just want a peaceful life without any chaos, and I hope now that everything has been cleared, we all can lead a peaceful life without any interruption, let's end everything here itself" Disha ended and looked in all the brothers eyes

Today she can say that even though she didn't hit the brothers or shouted at them or said even a thing which had slightest bit of malice in it, she has broke the brothers from inside

The great Raghuvanshi brothers who were cold hearted, aloof, rude, and always held their heads high, were now with their heads down with nothing escaping their mouths

Wiping her tears, Disha said for one last time before getting up

"If I have ever loved you at any point of my life, then let me tell you that I absolutely regret because it has brought nothing but pain in my life" she knows she told she won't say anything mean, but she needed this off her chest

Suddenly Raghav got up and said, his voice hoarse and nasal, indicating he was stopping himself from crying

"The thing we did was unforgivable and we would never ask for forgiveness, I know you would never need our help but if any point you feel like it, we can help-"

"After all it's not even the least we can do" Ryan completed it

"We don't want to leave with any grudge, so I won't say anything bad but just so you know, you are no more the people in our bad list, but it doesn't mean you would become good in our eyes, for now let's just stay as acquaintances" this was the first time that samaira wasn't talking with her fists with the brothers

Saying their goodbye, they all left, kritika was quite while all this, the girls also gave her space as she was still a little disturbed with Vedika's death

Once they reached their home, the boys opened the door, both sankalp and Hrithik, ran to them and all three of them, engulfed the two in a group hug

"You came back after so long my didu's, we missed you three so much" sankalp whined childishly

"We too my bandar"

"Harsh uncle didn't took care of us properly"Hritik complaint

"Hey you brat, I am still here"

Harsh just coming behind them, Harsh was the one who took care of Disha's brothers

There was still gloomy atmosphere, but the girls would never let it affect their brothers in any way, they will protect their brothers, what happened has happened, nothing could change it and

As if suddenly remembering something, Hritik suddenly ran inside and came back with something which was like a diary, he was holding in his hands

He stopped infront of Kritika, and shoved that diary in her hand and said, "Di a man came to deliver this diary and told someone has left the diary for you"

Kritika was shocked but seeing there was no harm in opening the diary, she unwrapped the thread which was secured around the diary and opening the cover she could see two sentences clearly

Vedika's DiaryDo not peek your nose in my business

Seeing this she was confused but she still decided to turn the pages and read the content to see what was there for her inside this diary

She flipped through different pages because it was all about her daily life and then she reached the last page

Kritika,I hope you are the one reading this, if yes then let me start first by apologizing, because I never wanted to be a antagonist in anyone's story but I guess this society can never see a boy and girl happily together just as friends

They always have to paint different pictures and force their labels on friends with opposite sex, you see I was naturally weak from childhood, and I always relied on those idiots who had pea-sized brain mostly on raghav

After getting up from induced coma, I realised that without even wanting to be one, I have became the villain in your love story, I knew you were the one who saved me from the accident and it was that Rishabh who drugged me and pushed me infront of your car to paint a your picture as a murderer infront of raghav

That's why I wanted you all to let the secrets of past be buried where they were, and never dug them out, because that Rishabh is more cruel than we can think but guess you all are indeed too brave and witty just like the brothers told me

Anyways I guess one more sorry won't hurt, so I am truly sorry

I hope this reaches you once I am no more in this world because I can't face you'll after this

P.s. sorry the time I pulled you in the storeroom but I need to say you have the best comebacks I just needed to see whether you even had a tiny bit of affection for that coconut head

The little note at the end made kritika chuckle, after reading the diary and telling everyone was inside of it, except sankalp and Hrithik of course, everyone was saddened thinking that Vedika too was just a misunderstood girl, the difference is that she just never told it out loud

"I guess it finally the end of our life drama"

But guess not, after few days Rishabh finally answered after being asked few times that why did the boys mother helped him kill his own husband and the only thing he answered with was

"That lady was in love with me and she killed him" and after that he didn't even utter a single sentence, spending rest of his life in the prison

But as this wasn't related to the girls anymore and the boys didn't wanted to burden them, the girls weren't even informed that the boys mother tried to commit suicide on her way to prison but in the end she was saved by the officers and now she would also spend rest of her life behind the bars

But for the girls this was really the end of drama....

[Nine years later]

"Navya, Kiana, Kiara get you ass down here and get your breakfast done" Samaira shouted as kept all the food on the table

All three of them ran downstairs, and started hurrying up because they all were late for their school, while dhvani the youngest among them was quietly having her breakfast while being all ready for her school

"You three never learn, always being late for school and making me and your other two moms late too for school"

That's right these four were their children

They all were their and the brothers children, well basically they were just the sperm donor and had done it through IVF

They could have adopted the babies too, and its not like they would have loved the adopted ones any less, but like every other woman they also wanted to experience the feeling when you become a mother, and carry your babies for months before giving them birth

The brothers were ready to do it and donate their sperms as they have already said that they would help them whenever the girls wanted and they did, after all it was such a small wish

In all this year, their animosity has decreased and they even meet each other as a friendly acquaintances, whenever they see each other

Samaira is now a lot more tolerant of them and now she doesn't throw her hands at them whenever she sees them, especially rudransh

Disha and Ryan, well they are better than before, Ryan visits her cafe which is now well known across the country and she has opened 5 more branches at different places and it has been getting more popular, and whenever she gets time she would drop lunches at his office

Kritika and Raghav, are as better as they could be, over the course of year, kritika was a lot less, you can say repulsive towards him, while raghav he tried not to anger her while he kept buying her art which was personally made by her

Oh and have I mentioned that Samaira is still going on with her classes while she is now a well known actress, known for her wonderful action films and her unbeatable fighting scenes

Kritika too is now a well known painter who sells her art and earns well and she is till going on with her studio of arts

Their current situation is as best as it can be and they could provide their kids with everything and anything they need

Oh, and Hritik and sankalp both went abroad to complete their higher studies, still every weekend they call to see their beautiful nieces and their gorgeous sister

Harsh was now settled abroad with his lover, yes he already had a stable job there, they still remember that he told them, 'he doesn't want to stay in a place where he is reminded of what his father has done and get guilty because of it everytime'

They tried to persuade him to stay but he was adamant to leave but he comes once in a while with his lover, but what made them astonished after seeing his lover was that his lover was not a 'she' but 'he'

They looked at him with a question on their face and then he said,

"Come one guys, I am a bi, don't look like that, and who wouldn't fall for such a wonderful person" he said while kissing him

They were happy for him and his boyfriend, Aaron, just like harsh said he was a sweet and wonderful guy and all four of them quickly bonded, and everytime harsh and Aaron came to India, harsh would sulk because neither his friends nor his lover would pay attention to him

Everything was going well and they didn't had anything to complain about

Today was Friday, and today was the day, all the ladies, the kids and the brothers would have dinner together in the mansion owned by the sisters...

The girls decided they would not hold back the kids to meet their fathers, and the kids text their fathers from time to time, so they are not totally a stranger, but they still don't have that strong bond as they had with their mothers

The kids thought that if they are family then why don't they stay together like the parents of the kids from their school, but their moma told them that they will answer this question once they reach the right age

"So how's the school going kids" Rudransh asked with a smile

"It's great" Kiana the most energetic one answered

"It nice to hear that" Ryan said

"Anyone giving you girls trouble at school?" Raghav asked, even though he have kept tabs on them to see if everything is going well with them in the school, he wanted them to tell him

"No dad everything is great, and if by chance anything is wrong I will show them who they are messing with" Kiana said

"Okay my little fighter, let's just eat food for now shall we" Kritika smiled and scolded at the same time

And looks like this was the dinner between them wasn't awkward or overbearing but this might be the dinner which was, peaceful

Standing near the balcony's railing were two people, side by side leaning on the railing, supporting their body while keeping their eyes straight still keeping tracks of each other movements

"Looks like we all had finally got over our past things, over the years everything has finally diminished, I can't believe we finally had a peaceful dinner, it feels good" Kritika smiled

"Yeah it does" Raghav answered

Turning towards him, while he did the same they both looked in each other's eyes, she mumbled

"Can I get a hug?" And she was engulfed in one, with no questions

Hugging was no big deal for both of them, once all the three sisters got pregnant at the same time, the brothers were the one who took care of them, while the nurse were also there (hired by the brothers) to look out for the ladies, if they are not there, you can say it was one of the reason all six of them got close,

But they can only go as far as being friends with the brothers, because they had their chance and they lost it, the ladies didn't have such a strong heart to take all of it again

"Sometimes I think whether if we were in different circumstances, would we have been different?" Raghav voiced out

"Instead of thinking of what could have happened if things went differently we should focus on what are having today, you should be grateful you are getting to hold someone who you have hurt so much, we can go as fas as friends, and right now I am tired, that's why I wanted a hug, now just shut up" after making him quite, they both separated from the hug and then the brothers left, the other two were also talking to their ex wives, they always do this

Talking with them and catching up on general stuffs and that's how over the course of year they have builded what you can call... Friendship

Even though the girls own such a big mansion, they all sleep together and the room they always choose is of Disha as she had queen sized bed which can fit all of them easily

Disha layed in the middle while kritika on her left and samaira on her right, they both cuddling her from each side while all of them staring at the ceiling

"What they say is true, no matter how much pain you get in life, everything is always solved in the end" Disha spoke

"It's true" kritika agreed

"Hmm I agree, the pain and the hardwork that we did payed in the end, I just pray that God gives our daughter immense happiness"

"Of course and along with god we will make sure of it too" kritika said

"Okay let's sleep, good night my babies"

"Good night Di" Kritika and samaira smiled and said at the same time, and hugged their Di tighter and slept soundly....

-The end-

www.ingramcontent.com/pod-product-compliance
Lightning Source LLC
Chambersburg PA
CBHW071428200726
48294CB00002B/559